The Horse-Tamer

Professor William Dailey claimed he could cure *any* horse of biting, kicking, balking, running away, throwing himself over backwards, shying at umbrellas, at baby carriages or at anything else. For Dailey was a professional horse-tamer.

Many years ago almost every family had a horse, yet few people knew how to handle the animals when they acted up. It was then that many owners turned to Dailey for help. But while he made friends at his work, Dailey also made many enemies—men who called him a humbug, a magician or even a wizard who fleeced the public by using "secret" taming potions!

The Horse-Tamer is a story told by the trainer of the Black Stallion to young Alec Ramsay, and Alec listened intently—for it's an exciting story of an unusual man.

The Horse-Tamer

by *WALTER FARLEY*

illustrated by James Schucker

RANDOM HOUSE  **NEW YORK**

Library of Congress Cataloging in Publication Data

Farley, Walter
The horse-tamer
New York, Random House [1958]
I. Title   PZ7.F236Ho   58-9030
ISBN:0-394-80614-X (trade hardcover)
0-394-90614-4 (library binding)
0-394-84374-6 (trade paperback)

*To the professional horseman
who helps others understand their
horses—and themselves—better*

Contents

The Horse-Tamer

A World of Horses

1

The old man's hair was as silver as the glistening wings of the plane; the youth's as red as the sun beyond the runway. The two of them stepped back quickly as the inboard engines caught, blasting the air. Above the even rumble the old man asked anxiously, "You're sure the Black's all right, Alec?"

"Positive, or I wouldn't have left him alone. When do we take off?"

"Not for a long while, I'm afraid. The chief mechanic said this is just routine preflight inspection. We're not goin' anywhere yet. We got trouble above."

"Trouble above?" Alec repeated wonderingly.

They looked at the sky together. It was soft, cloudless and empty.

"*Traffic* trouble, Alec. They've run out of air space."

"It doesn't look that way from down here."

"No, but they got avenues up there an' they go right across the Atlantic. They're jammed. The tower told the chief mechanic that a Pan Am and a TWA flight are coming in fifteen minutes apart. And there's a flight of air force jets behind 'em."

"You picked up a lot of information, Henry."

"I listen to 'em gab. They said it'll be at least two hours before we're cleared for takeoff."

"Imagine running out of air space," Alec said incredulously.

"Imagine bein' able to fly from Lisbon to New York in a matter of a few hours!" Henry echoed. "That's what gets me." His gaze returned to the airplane. Just a big hunk of metal going nowhere in particular, he mused—nowhere but across the Atlantic Ocean, or some two thousand miles of open water, carrying over three thousand gallons of gas and seventy thousand pounds of cargo, including them and their black horse. It was a fast-moving world, all right!

"I'm going back to the stable," Alec said.

"Me too. I'm more at home there," the old man replied.

Henry Dailey, who was in his sixty-second year of

training and racing horses, followed Alec Ramsay
around the airport administration building to a large
livestock shed in the rear. He listened affectionately
to the sounds of the penned and stabled animals.
Most of them he recognized easily—the bawling
calves, some pigs, an unhappy dog and of course the
Black.

"But what's that chattering going on down at the
far end?" he asked Alec.

"Monkeys," the boy answered. "They must have
twenty of 'em in cages. Bound for U.S. zoos, the
barn super said."

With the opening of his stall door the Black
Stallion came forward quickly, his eyes alert and
impatient.

"Not yet. Not yet, but soon," Alec told him softly.

The old trainer watched the Black dance in the
straw, noting how much he favored his right
forefoot. He had suffered a severe stone bruise in
Europe and there'd be no racing him for a while.
One didn't take chances with this kind of a horse.
That's why they were going home.

Henry noted, too, that the famous stallion's coat
shone as brightly as his eyes. While waiting for the
plane's departure Alec had groomed him to within
an inch of his life. His small ears were pricked,
catching the strange sounds from the other animals.

His fine head was held high. His every sense was alert. Every muscle, every sinew was ready to be unleashed with the power and swiftness of a coiled steel spring. The Black was all horse.

Nothing will ever take his place, the trainer thought. *No multi-engined plane or jet, no rocket or missile or spaceship. There's always been need for a fine horse. There always will be. Or am I just an old fool to go on thinking so?*

Henry Dailey bent down to the straw, carefully picking up the horse's injured foot. *How many thousands of feet have I picked up, I wonder?* he asked himself. *How many thousands of days and nights have I spent at it?* Someday he might figure it out. Just for the laughs.

Alec asked anxiously, "It's better, isn't it, Henry?"

"You asked me that only this morning," the trainer replied brusquely. "It's no better, Alec, no better at all. An injury like this takes time to heal. You *got* to be patient."

"I *am* patient," Alec said quickly, sensitive to the old man's sharp criticism. "I've got time, plenty of time . . . so has he. I was just asking."

Henry put down the Black's foot. "Have a seat then," he said more kindly, patting the straw beside him, "and let's stop rushin' from country to country

an' from race to race. It's snug an' warm here and
we have a fine horse to look at. What more could we
want?"

"There!" Alec said, dropping to the straw beside
the old man. "This is the life, all right," he agreed,
laughing easily because he was very content.

"Yep, and I want to tell you a little more about
this kind of life. It just might be that horses are goin'
out of fashion." Henry's eyes weren't on Alec but on
the oval-shaped hoofs buried in the straw. "Some of
the things that have happened to horses might be
forgotten with the world movin' fast like it is."

A strange, excited note came into the old man's
voice as he asked suddenly, "Did you ever hear of a
professional horse-tamer, Alec?"

"Trainer, you mean, Henry? Like you are?"

"No. *Tamer*."

"No, then. Lion-tamer, yes. Horse-tamer, no.
Did he use a long whip and snap it in a ring?" Alec
asked with attempted lightness.

"Sometimes," Henry answered seriously. "The
whip was one of the tools of his trade and occasionally he had good use for it. There was a need for
such men just before the turn of the century. The
big trouble was that there weren't enough of them
to go around. Most everybody had a horse, y'know.
It was about the only way of gettin' from place to

place. Yet few owners knew anything about horses except how to ride or drive 'em. When trouble arose, it was hard on both man and horse. That's when they started lookin' around for a horse-tamer."

Henry paused and Alec said, "They could have called him a trainer. A tamer makes you think of *wild* animals."

"Training takes time, Alec, as you know, and these men had no time. They did a job in a matter of hours—a few days at most—and then went on to the next case. Some of the horses, too, were worse than wild animals—vicious, mean horses. Most often, of course, they were the result of bad handling by their owners. But come to think of it, what kind of a job would you and I do on that plane outside? We're no mechanics and, as I say, so many owners in the old days weren't horsemen. They just needed a horse to get around. They made mistakes, plenty of 'em—and they suffered for it. So did their horses."

Alec chewed thoughtfully on a piece of straw. He was beginning to understand what Henry was getting at. He could imagine thousands upon thousands of horses developing bad habits and vices, most of them going from bad to worse because their owners had no professional ability or help. One horse kicked; a second balked; a third

pulled against the bit and ran away; a fourth would
not stand still to wait or to be shod or to be
mounted; another would not back up; still others
would bite or rear or throw themselves over
backwards or refuse to work. Then again they would
be afraid of umbrellas, blankets, carts, wagons,
cows, baby carriages or something else. With all
this happening in crowded city streets where horses
were the sole means of transportation, people could
be hurt or killed and property destroyed.

"Were you ever a horse-tamer?" Alec asked
Henry.

"No, but my oldest brother was. I watched him at
it. He was good."

"How good?"

"One of the best," the old man answered, his
eyes bright with memories. "Bill was about thirty, I
guess, when my father sent me off one summer to
live with him. That was back in Pennsylvania. I was
just a kid but not too young to learn a trade. . . ."

"You mean that horse-taming trade?"

"No, not that. Bill wasn't in it then. He was a
carriage-maker and a good one." Henry laughed. "I
remember that he always called me Hank an' I
didn't like the nickname at all."

"So you became a carriage-maker," Alec commented.

"Not at all. Turned out that I didn't learn a thing
about carriage making. I remember that first day
pretty well. We were deliverin' a new buggy Bill
had just finished to a Mr. Murray. . . ."
And then Henry went on with the story.

The carriage was designed for speed as well as
elegance and it matched the sleek bay trotter up
front. The long shafts were made of ash, beautifully
polished and varnished. The wheels were rubber-
tired and caught the sun's rays with their shiny
brass inner rings, red spokes and nickled hubs. The
patent-leather dashboard was flanked on each side
by a brass lamp studded with large red-glass rubies.
The whip-socket was made of silver plate. The top
of the carriage, of soft yellow leather, could be
removed completely during fair weather. The seat
was luxurious, with deep springs for easy riding,
and had a wicker shoulder-rest.

"Mr. Murray might not like you deliverin' his
new buggy this way, Bill," the boy warned, sitting
nervously on the edge of his seat.

"You got no cause to worry, Hank," his brother
replied. "If he says anything, it'll be to me. An' as
long as I get his new buggy to him in good order
what difference does it make *how* I deliver it?"

"You could at least have put some kind of a bridle

on this horse. The time to practice drivin' without reins is when you have your own buggy."

"I practice with *any* buggy, *any* time. You'd better get used to that if you plan to stick around, Hank."

"I came to learn how to make carriages, not do tricks," the boy said, "especially tricks that can get you into trouble."

The man tried unsuccessfully to blow a lock of

long black hair away from his eyes. "You'll learn both," he said, laughing, "an' you won't get into trouble either. You jus' stick with your big brother Bill. He'll take care of you, all right. Get up there, you lazy old mare! Pepper up!"

Bill Dailey turned the horse into a long driveway without benefit of bridle or reins. He carried only a long whip with which he had tapped the mare lightly on the off shoulder just before the turn. Not content with this remarkable feat he tapped her again, this time turning her completely around.

"You're goin' to upset us," the boy warned.

"You're worse than an old maid," the man said, straightening out the mare with another touch of his whip. As they went down the lane he sent her first to the left and then to the right with ease.

"You haven't got paid for this buggy yet," the boy reminded him. "An' I got a feelin' you won't be."

The man grinned. "I sure will, Hank. We've only got a half mile to go." He sent the mare into a hard trot.

"Are you goin' to be able to stop her?" The dust and dirt were flying behind them.

"Yep," the man answered. "This trick's nothin', Hank. The mare makes it easy, just the kind for driving without reins. She's smart but lazy and gentle. She's not the kind to run away." He tapped

the back of the mare's head and she slowed
immediately to a walk. "See!" he said, pleased with
himself and the mare. "How about that?"

The boy nodded and glanced at the lovely fenced
fields on either side of them.

"Nothin' hurried here, ever," Bill Dailey told his
brother.

"Is that why you slowed her down to a walk, to
make less noise?"

"Yep."

"Bill . . ."

"Yeah?"

"Will you teach me how to drive without reins?"

"You really want to learn?"

The boy nodded self-consciously, recalling his
earlier criticism.

"Even more than makin' carriages?" the man
asked teasingly.

"*Anyone* can make carriages, Bill."

"All right, Hank," the man said seriously. "Now
you're talkin' the way I like to hear. It's an easy
trick. The secret's all in pickin' the right horse. I'd
like to teach you. I'd like to teach you a lot of things
about horses."

Bill Dailey slowed the bay mare still more. "The
only runnin' Mr. Murray allows around here," he
said, "is what's done by the foals. He never likes a

horse to be startled. They just lap up peace and quiet. He's got them thinkin' the world is theirs. Not a sound, not ever a . . ."

The sharp crack of a whip shattered the quiet summer air. It came from around a bend in the drive. A man bellowed angrily. Again the whip cracked . . . again and again and again.

Frightened by the sounds, their bay mare jumped and swerved, almost upsetting the buggy. As she swept down the road Bill was already on his feet, trying to stop her with his long whip. He tapped her lightly on the back of the head and she was responding to his urgent command when one of the wheels caught in a deep rut. The buggy tipped, then slid abruptly to one side, crashing hard against a bordering tree. There was a shattering of red-spoked wheels, ruby glass and polished wood, and the smart yellow top came down heavily.

Man and boy scrambled to the ground and went to the bay mare's head. She was frightened and shaken but not hurt.

"You all right?" Bill asked his brother anxiously.

"Yeah, but take a good look at Mr. Murray's new buggy."

The man's eyes didn't leave the mare. "She'd have stopped if I'd gotten to her before this tree did. It wasn't her fault. She—" He stopped as if

suddenly recalling the cause of their accident and
swept his gaze down the lane.

In the middle of the road was a peddler's wagon,
its flat-bed laden and bulging with glistening pails,
tinware, clocks, muslins, taffetas, lightning rods,
bells, books and bull rings. There were also patent
medicines, jewelry, bright scarves, handkerchiefs,
needles and thread; boots, shoes, chewing gum and
tobacco; linoleum, Bibles and buggy whips.

The shafts of the wagon were empty and the
horse was tied to a tree. He was a young colt, gray
and of medium size. The peddler, flushed and
exhausted, stood a few feet away with a buggy whip
in his hand, his fine coat and stovepipe hat lying
neatly on the ground.

"You'll kill yourself and your colt too," Bill Dailey
called to him.

The peddler was large, almost a colossus of a man;
his hair was fair and unruly, and his face handsome
and unlined. He could have made two of Bill
Dailey. He laughed wildly as he took in the thin,
almost slight figure of the stranger who seemed so
concerned about him and his colt when he had just
had an accident himself.

"Thank you, sir," he said finally, "but this is a bad
one, he is. As bad, I'm sure, as your runaway."
There was an Irish lilt to the peddler's voice. "He

either balks or lunges. One minute he won't go. The next I can't stop him. He's the worst I've ever had."

"Whipping won't cure him," Bill said, walking over. "He's got nerve and courage. He'll take your whipping until he drops . . . or until you do."

The peddler grinned. "You got a real sense of duty to warn me, stranger." He had suddenly changed his mind about this man. The fellow might be thin but he seemed made of steel. "Now what do you suggest I do?" he asked.

"Let me take him over," Bill answered, thoroughly at ease despite the towering hulk beside him.

"You?" the peddler asked suspiciously. "You seem to have your own troubles." He eyed the bay mare beyond without realizing that she wore neither bridle nor reins.

"I'll loan you a horse until I'm done with yours," Bill said, ignoring the big man's remark. "It'll take me a couple of days. Your colt must have had bad treatment long before you got him."

"How do you know?"

"I'm lookin' at him, that's how I know." Bill's tone was self-reliant, confident. It made up for his want of size. "It's my business to know," he added.

The peddler frowned in perplexity. "What business are you in, anyway? Horse dealing?"

"No, carriage making," Bill answered. He turned
to look back at his brother and the shattered buggy.
"That is, I *was* in it," he added. "I'm not so sure
now. Anyway, you come to my shop in Birdsboro
and I'll loan you a horse that you won't need to use a
whip on."

"How do you know I won't run out on you?" the
peddler asked, grinning.

"You're leavin' too good a colt behind and you
know I'm goin' to straighten him out for you, that's
why."

The peddler noted the look of cold command in
the other's eyes. "Yes, I know that, all right. But
don't ask me how I know it." He threw down the
buggy whip and offered his hand good-naturedly.
"My name's Caspersen, Finn Caspersen."

"Mine's Bill Dailey. An' over there is my kid
brother Hank."

"Want me to come along to your shop now?" the
peddler asked a little nervously. He didn't like
being made to feel uneasy. He decided, too, that he
wouldn't want to come to blows with Bill Dailey
despite his small size.

"Yes, we'll hitch up my mare to your wagon and
lead the colt," Bill answered.

"What about your buggy?"

"I'll come back for it later."

"Maybe you can fix it up," the big man suggested hesitantly.

"Maybe I can. But first I want to fix up your colt. He's young an' he's had some bad times." Bill Dailey's eyes were half-closed as he squinted in the bright sun.

The peddler put on his fine coat slowly. "You sure got a heap of feelin' for bad horses, Bill," he said almost in awe. "You sure have."

*Dried Osselets
and Apples*

2

Early the next morning Bill took his brother into the
apple orchard behind his carriage shop.

"Some horsemen say," he told Hank, "that the
best remedy for a balker like this colt is to take
osselets, or small bones, from his legs, dry and grate
them fine, then blow a thimbleful into his nostrils.
He'll then go off without trouble." Bill picked
several apples and put them into his pockets. "But
I've had better luck with these," he added, laughing.

"But will the dried osselets work?" Hank asked
curiously.

"About like ammonia or red pepper. They're only
temporary aids. They disconcert a balker long

enough to get him to start, but they don't *keep* him goin'."

A few minutes later Bill led the gray colt, wearing harness, down a back road. He stopped and started him repeatedly, each time rewarding the colt with a bit of apple and stroking his neck and head.

"There's nothin' wrong with this colt that some kindness won't help," he told Hank. "Winning a young horse's confidence is always the first step. This fellow's had too much abuse."

Bill untied the long reins from the harness and for the first time stood a little to the side and rear of the colt. "Now, boy," he said, tapping him lightly over the hips, "get along, an' do the same thing you been doin' with me up front."

The colt moved off smartly and continued down the road until commanded to stop. He looked around and Bill gave him a bit of apple and a pat on the head. Then he was sent off once more until a touch of the reins brought him to another halt.

After repeating this many times with no trouble, Bill said, "Now for my wagon, Hank."

They hitched up the colt and he immediately began to fret.

"He's afraid of it," Bill said, "an' now we'll try to find out why. If we do, curin' him of balkin' won't be any trick at all."

"The peddler had a big load," Hank reminded his brother. "Maybe he was overloaded and the colt refused to pull."

"Overloading wouldn't cause fear," Bill said.

"Maybe the crosspiece struck his legs once," Hank suggested, trying his best to be helpful.

Bill Dailey slid a pole over the gray haunches but the colt neither kicked nor made any effort to break away. Finally Bill touched him with the reins. For a second the colt hesitated and Bill urged soothingly, "Easy, boy, get along with you now."

The colt took a single stride and the wheels of the empty wagon turned noiselessly behind him. As he took another stride, and still another, Bill walked alongside but a little to the rear, talking to the colt all the while. Hank followed.

They could see the colt's confidence return as he moved in the stillness of the early morning. His fine body stopped trembling and only the backward flicking of his ears indicated his concern for what was going on behind him. Bill stopped him repeatedly, rewarding him each time with a bit of apple, and then going on again. Finally Bill started for home.

"It's got to be Caspersen's wagon he's afraid of," Bill told his brother. "There's nothin' wrong with him while he's pullin' mine."

"Maybe it's not so much Caspersen's wagon as what's in it," Hank suggested. He wanted very much to be helpful, for in a way that's why he was here. Before long he'd have to make his own way in life just as Bill was doing. He'd have to face the realities of an adult world alone. Bill would help prepare him to meet this new and sometimes terrifying challenge.

"Think of all the merchandise Caspersen sells," the boy went on eagerly. "Think of the buffalo robes an'—"

"I am thinkin' of them," Bill interrupted, his eyes half-closed. "This wouldn't be the first horse to be frightened by a buffalo robe or an umbrella. You might be right at that, Hank."

"Or maybe bright scarves scare him," the boy put in quickly. "Or it could be the lightning rods, bells, books, bull rings, tinware . . ."

Bill Dailey nodded in agreement as his brother went on breathlessly. He was pleased with Hank. He was pleased with all he saw in the bright, deep-set eyes. Hank was growing up fast, and already was as tall as he. His weight was distributed like their father's—solid through the shoulders, back and chest. Hank probably wouldn't get much bigger, none of them did—and they were seven, all boys. He'd be a natural leader, too. Hank was the youngest of them all, but his smaller size hadn't stopped him from holding his own during their childish games and roughhousing, his body straining and weaving in competition against theirs. They were a closely knit family even though, there being so many of them, it was economically necessary for them to leave home early in search of work. But no number of miles would ever destroy the firm and joyful allegiance they had for each other.

Bill knew exactly why his father had sent Hank to him this summer. And he was aware of his responsibility in setting a good example, for Hank would watch everything he did with quiet, reverent eyes.

". . . and don't forget those buggy whips," Hank was concluding excitedly. "Maybe he'd been beaten and just the sight of them—"

"No," Bill answered. "I don't think we'll find it's whips he's scared of. Although I do know Caspersen made matters a lot worse by beating him when he balked. Nope, Hank, this colt's scared of something besides whips. It's something simple and we're goin' to find out what it is."

Back at the stable Hank asked, "What do you want me to do, Bill?" His voice was eager but respectful, the younger toward the older. "I can find some of the things that were in the wagon. We can try them one at a time. . . ."

"No, Hank, we won't need many. That is, I hope we won't."

"But you said—"

"I said we'd find out what's scarin' this colt an' we will," Bill interrupted. "But look at it this way. He not only balks but he runs away. One moment Caspersen can't start him an' the next he can't stop him. So I figure it might have more to do with *noise* than things."

"You mean the rattling of all that tinware maybe?" Hank asked.

Bill Dailey nodded. "It makes more sense to me that way. First the colt won't go because if he does the noise behind him starts up. And for some reason he's afraid of it. So when he's *made* to go, he runs away tryin' to get clear of it."

They gathered all the stable pails they could find and put them in the back of the wagon. From the moment one pail clanged against another the colt became uneasy. At first there were only little spots of perspiration on his gray coat but later, as Bill Dailey intentionally banged the pails against each other, white lather appeared between the colt's hind legs. He began digging into the dirt road with his right foreleg.

When Bill Dailey took up the reins and clucked, the colt wouldn't budge. "There's our balker," Bill said quietly.

"The noise made by Capersen's pails and tinware

is our answer then," Hank added. "But why is he scared, Bill?"

"I don't know, and it's not important just now. All we need to do is to teach him that he has nothin' to fear from such noise."

"Maybe he stepped in a pail and hurt himself once," Hank suggested.

"Maybe he did. It's happened before." But the man wasn't talking to the boy. His words were for the colt and they were as soft and kind as his hands. He rubbed him and soothed him, humming all the while, and then he gave him an apple.

Later he removed all the pails from the wagon and, slinging one over an arm, returned to the colt. The animal fastened frightened eyes on the pail but Bill ignored it completely, merely continuing to talk soothingly to him. Soon he got the colt to take one step forward and then another. Finally he was able to walk him up and down the road, the pail swinging lightly between them. The colt's eyes never left it but no longer did he perspire in the cool morning air.

By noon Bill Dailey was able to drop the pail on the road without upsetting the colt. Still later in the day he was kicking it, sending it along with loud and seemingly never-ending clanks. When the colt had become so accustomed to the noise that he ignored

the pail completely, Bill told his brother that he felt
their work was done.

Throwing the pail into the wagon, he picked up
the reins. "Now, boy," he said, "let's go home!"

The colt went down the road at a hard trot, the
pail rattling and the dust and dirt rising in his wake.

Finn Caspersen returned the following afternoon
and the gray colt was hitched up to his loaded
wagon. He drove noisily down the road and back,
stopping and starting at will. Finally he said in
amazement, "Dailey, I wouldn't have believed this
possible. What did you do to him? What system did
you use?"

"My own," Bill answered, smiling faintly. "A few
apples and a pat on the head."

The big man removed his stovepipe hat. "Be
honest with me, sir! I know nothing about horses
except how to drive them in the course of my work
but I would pay five dollars to learn what you did!"

"It's not worth five dollars," Bill protested. "Your
colt was afraid of all the noise your pots, pans an'
pails made. I showed him that he needn't be. That's
all there was to it. Trouble is, mister, you didn't
even take the time to find out."

Finn Caspersen drew himself up to his full
height. He didn't relish being criticized so sharply.

"Pails, pots and pans you say?" he asked finally,
regaining his professional composure. "Now that

you mention pails I recall . . ." He paused to run a big hand through his unruly hair. "It most certainly does fit very well with what you have told me." He paused again, this time breaking out into hearty laughter before he went on.

"I remember this colt as a weanling," Caspersen said with the air of one about to tell a good story. "He belonged to a friend in Harrisburg who had no pasture. Since the colt was very friendly he was allowed to go grazing on people's lawns. They all got to thinking of him as they would a big dog. But one old man in the neighborhood got sore and tied a big tin pail to his tail to frighten him off. The colt was all right until he moved; then when the pail started rattling and thumping against his heels it scared the daylights out of him and he took off. The faster he ran the worse it became. I don't know how they ever caught up with him."

As he finished Finn Caspersen became uneasy and his gaze shifted from Bill Dailey to the boy standing alongside. "Of course, I'd forgotten all about it. It was a long time ago."

"But the colt didn't forget," Bill said quietly.

"I realize that now. Should have thought of it, of course. But that's not the way my mind runs. Say, it didn't take you long to figure it out, though!" He slapped Bill on the shoulder, glancing around the stable yard as he did so. "It occurs to me, sir, that you're in the wrong business. You seem to have more horses around here than carriages."

Bill Dailey shrugged. "That's because I've been trading carriages for horses," he answered, slightly amused by Caspersen's criticism. "They had bad habits, all of them. I guess that's how we got together. They needed help and I traded for 'em."

"You should *sell* what you know, sir," the big man went on persuasively. "If it's worth five dollars to me it's worth the same to a lot of other people."

"I'm a carriage-maker," Bill answered, with a sudden rush of pride in his craft. "Last year I took first prize at two county fairs in Berks, first for a single carriage, the second for a double."

"You do all the work yourself?" Caspersen asked. "All the painting and trimming? You do that, too?"

"Yep."

"And you think you'll be able to compete with the big carriage manufacturers much longer? Have you been in that new Studebaker Brothers store over in Pottstown? Why, sir, they're giving door prizes just for going in and *looking* at their wagons! How can you compete against a big firm like that? And have you seen the special buggy Sears, Roebuck is selling for $54.70?" he asked hurriedly. "You haven't? Look here, then!"

Pulling a huge catalog from behind the wagon

seat, Finn Caspersen opened it to page 692 and shoved it into Bill Dailey's arms. "Are you going to be able to compete against the 'Cheapest Supply House on Earth,' sir? Are you?"

SEARS, ROEBUCK & CO., (INCORPORATED), CHEAPEST SUPPLY HOUSE ON EARTH, CHICAGO
OUR SPECIAL $54.70 JUMP SEAT BUGGY

JUST SEND US $5.00 and we will send you the buggy to your nearest railroad station to examine.

"No, I can't make a carriage for that," Bill admitted calmly but with some of the sadness, too, of a man whose bridges were being burned behind him. He flipped over the hundreds of pages displaying all kinds of merchandise before handing the catalog back to Caspersen. "Any more than *you* can sell your things cheaper."

Finn Caspersen said agreeably, "That's right, sir, but I have other ways of earning a living—and so have *you*." He paused for effect, then continued in a confidential, friendly tone. "There's a farmer over in Pottstown who has a mare that bites worse than any horse I've ever seen. It's worth ten dollars to him to get her cured. I've heard him say so a dozen times. You could do it for him, Bill. You sure could."

"I'd be glad to help him out," Bill said. "But I don't want his money."

"Let me take care of that end," Finn Caspersen said hastily. "You just take care of his mare. Let me worry about everything else."

"She shouldn't be bitin' like you say," Bill mused. "She'll hurt somebody bad if she isn't taught to stop."

"That's what I was hoping you'd say, Bill. You'll take her on, then?"

"Somebody ought to help her or she'll get herself into a peck of trouble."

"Somebody sure had, Bill. Will it be you? Will it?"

"All right. Tomorrow. I got time to do it tomorrow."

Wild Bess

3

"I must warn you," the Pottstown farmer said, "that she's the most vicious, biting mare known in this end of the county. When turned loose, she runs at a man with all the ferocity of a bulldog. I would've got rid of her long ago if I hadn't paid so much for her."

He finished milking his cows and concluded, "We'll have some breakfast and then go see her."

"We've eaten," Bill Dailey said impatiently. "I'd like to get started. I got work at home. That's why we came so early."

The farmer smiled. "You cure my mare like Mr. Caspersen says you can an' it'll be enough work for one day. Fifty dollars is a lot of money for a day's work."

"F-Fifty dollars?" Bill stammered unbelievingly.

Finn Caspersen explained. "I suggested to Mr. Boyer that he gather ten of his neighbors, at five dollars each, to watch your performance, Bill. You will then be giving instruction to ten persons at a nominal charge. You might say," he added, "that you are about to conduct your first class in horse taming."

"I'm no horse-tamer," Bill protested. "I just want to help out Mr. Boyer."

"And that you'll be doing, son," the farmer said, "if you can handle her."

"Did she bite when you bought her?" Bill asked, wanting to get back to the mare.

"Just nipped, but she went from bad to worse. I couldn't do anything with her."

"Did you try?" Bill asked.

The farmer shifted uneasily. "Not often. You see, it became too dangerous to approach her. I had no choice but to leave her alone. I even had to feed her from above."

"Y'mean you left her alone in her stall?" Bill asked incredulously. "Y'never even took her out?"

"It's a large stall," Mr. Boyer said defensively. "She has plenty of room, as you'll see for yourself. You don't need to feel sorry for her."

Bill shook his head. "But you encouraged her to resist control," he said. "No wonder she's become vicious."

"I'm a farmer," the man replied, "not a horse-tamer. I expect obedience from my animals and not a fight every time I go near them."

"Obedience has to be taught," Bill pointed out, "or encouraged, anyway. You've done nothing for this mare."

"And what will *you* do?" the farmer asked sharply. He was becoming irritated by Bill Dailey's criticism and self-reliant air.

"First, I've got to teach her all over again that she can be controlled. You've made resistance very exciting to her."

The farmer grinned. "I suspect you're goin' to find it pretty exciting yourself, son. It'll be worth the money just to watch the show you an' Wild Bess put on."

"I'm not puttin' on any show," Bill replied quietly. "What I do for your mare will only be the beginning. Once I get her used to bein' handled again you've got to treat her right. She's got to get over whatever resentment she's built up against people. You can do it just as easy as you made biting an exciting game for her. Win her confidence by good, kind handling. It won't take long. It never does."

"You get her so she can be handled and I'll take care of the rest," the farmer retorted. "You talk good but I'm wonderin' just how far you're going to get with Wild Bess."

When they returned to the barn a little later, Mr. Boyer's neighbors were awaiting them. One man eyed the thin cord Bill Dailey carried in his hand and said, "'Pears to me you're goin' to be needing a lot more than that, mister."

"At least a ten-foot pole," another joined in, laughing. "I guess he's never seen Wild Bess, hey, boys?"

They went to the second floor of the barn, where there was a large entryway flanked by haymows. A box stall could be seen at the far end.

"You'll have plenty of room here," the farmer said, sliding shut the two large barn doors behind them.

Bill nodded, meanwhile watching Mr. Boyer's neighbors climb the rungs of a ladder to sit on a high beam. "You'd better get up there, too," he told his brother and Finn Caspersen.

"Are you sure you don't want a pole?" Wild Bess's owner asked. "She's not even wearin' a halter."

"Then I'll need a slip-noose halter," Bill replied. "That's all. Then you can go too. I'll open the door myself."

A few minutes later he walked toward the stall. He was anxious to see Wild Bess for he had learned to associate a horse's disposition and character with its color, eyes, ears and contours. He wasn't often wrong, and knowing what to expect gave him an advantage over the animal.

Reaching the stall, Bill Dailey looked inside and knew immediately that Mr. Boyer had not been exaggerating the mare's ferocity.

Wild Bess moved about her stall with the grace of a cat. Her medium size told him she'd be wonderfully quick, and by the shape of her head he knew she'd make few mistakes in the coming struggle. She was finely boned, with thin skin and a small chest. She was not inclined to put on flesh—in other words, she was the kind of horse he'd found to be very sensitive and active but with little stamina. Resistance and bad habits in this type most often came from excitement rather than inherent viciousness. Wild Bess had had her own way too long but should respond readily to good management.

As Bill spoke to her through the bars of the stall, he hoped he was correct in his analysis. Within a few minutes he would know—for it might mean success or failure in handling her. He noted once more her large brown eyes, and the thin lids. Her forehead was broad and her nostrils extra large.

An intelligent mare, one that would quickly learn good habits or bad. On the other hand she was a sorrel and the most vicious horses he had ever handled were of that color or a dull iron-gray or black. She moved faster about the stall, aware of his presence and yet paying no attention to him. He knew that when the opportunity came she would strike without warning. It would be best to meet her head-on, hoping to win control almost immediately and ending the fight before it began.

Naturally, Wild Bess was stronger than he. The secret was not to let her know it. This mare would have to be treated like the bully she'd become. And the less time it took, the better; she'd been encouraged to resist control long enough. Bill opened the door, holding the rope halter Mr. Boyer had given him. If she had been wearing a halter, it would have made what he had to do a lot easier.

Wild Bess came out of the stall too fast for him to get the halter on her. She turned upon him, her teeth bared and ears laid back. He succeeded in knocking her mouth to one side and then jumped around her. She came after him again and he had no alternative but to run, seeking escape.

Directly ahead of him Bill saw a wooden partition. He grabbed the top rail, scrambling over it as the mare got hold of his pant leg. He heard it rip as he fell headlong into an empty mow which was another five feet below the barn floor. For a moment he lay still, catching his breath and listening to the loud laughter and jeers of the farmers above.

His brother called anxiously, "Bill, are you hurt?"

He got to his feet to show them he was all right. He listened to their taunts and tried to keep his temper. He had to stay calm if he was to win control over this mare. Class wasn't over, not yet, he wanted to tell them and Wild Bess. As he held the rope halter in his hand he noticed that there were some sticks on the floor of the mow. He selected a long one and, hanging the headpiece of the halter on it, unfastened the slip noose. He took hold of the dangling end, ready to take up the slack once he got the halter on Wild Bess's head.

The mare looked over the partition, watching him. With his long stick Bill raised the halter toward her and, when she tried to grab it, expertly slipped the large noose over her nose. Then, with a half-twist of the stick, he had the head part over and behind her ears. Quickly he pulled on the rope, taking up the slack and making the halter secure on Wild Bess.

She drew back hard but he had good leverage and held her with little trouble.

She came at him when he climbed to the top of the partition but Bill kept her away by shoving the end of the stick against her jaw. Jumping down onto the barn floor, he took as short a hold of the halter rope as he possibly could—but he still didn't know exactly what he was going to do to win control of the mare.

Suddenly Wild Bess reached for him, her head as pointed as a snake's. Bill jumped away, pulling her head around and staying close to her hindquarters. Her long tail cut the air and without thinking he grabbed the tail with his free hand and hung on. She spun him around and he barely kept on his feet as they made several tight circles.

He ran hard in an effort to stay with her, realizing that he couldn't let go of either halter rope or tail. If he did he'd be dragged under her hoofs. Worked up as she was, she wouldn't hesitate to strike as well as bite.

Around and around they whirled, Bill Dailey hoping desperately he'd been right in his estimate of her and that Wild Bess had little endurance. He kept his eyes wide open to keep from getting dizzy. The mare went around many times before there was any noticeable slowing of her turns. Finally she came to a stop, her eyes rolling, her legs unsteady.

Bill took advantage of her immobility by running around to the other side of her before catching hold of her tail again. Once more he pulled her head toward him, and this time he turned her slowly in reverse circles. She went around only a few times. Then she dropped to the barn floor, dizzy, dazed and helpless.

"Now Wild Bess is not so wild," Bill said,

breathing heavily. "We got one more thing to do, Bess, you and I, just one more thing." He took the long cord from his pants pocket and tied a hard knot at each end. Then he made a loop at one end and put it around the mare's neck, regulating the size so as not to get it too tight. Taking the other end of the cord, he drew it through the mare's mouth and back to the neck. Finally he passed it through the noose and pulled up the slack.

Now he had a bridle on Wild Bess and could control her. Bending down, he spoke to her kindly as he stroked her head. She listened to him and

made no attempt to bite. Finally he said, "Get up, Bess," at the same time applying slight pressure on the cord bridle he had fashioned.

When she was standing, Bill watched her carefully for any further signs of resistance. She neither bit the cord in her mouth nor struck at him with her forefeet. Wild Bess had the intelligence to learn quickly. With proper handling she would make just as good a mare as she had a bad one.

Bill Dailey knew there was nothing more he could do just then. The rest was up to Mr. Boyer. Raising his head, he looked up at the farmer, who was sitting with the others, and said, "Now, sir, will you come down and take your horse?"

The owner shook his head vigorously. "What assurance can you give me that you haven't tamed her only for *yourself*?"

For a moment Bill Dailey was puzzled. Then he called out to his young brother, "Hank, come down and take this mare."

All eyes turned to the boy as he went down to the barn floor. He looked strong and alert for his age but he was no match for Wild Bess if she should suddenly turn on him. This they fully expected her to do. But they could see that this boy was linked by blood to the man who had conquered Wild Bess. He had the same thrust to his jaw, and he walked on the balls of his feet with rapid, springy steps which took him quickly to the mare's side.

"I'll take her, Bill," they heard him say eagerly. There was no doubt that he was the kind of person who dreamed of doing great things. Still, he was just a boy and they were ashamed of their own fears when they saw him lead Wild Bess about the barn floor.

Bill Dailey, leaving them alone, turned his back upon the boy and horse and climbed to the high beam to sit beside Mr. Boyer. He didn't talk to the farmer or anyone else, and his eyes were filled with scorn.

Below on the barn floor, Hank Dailey continued to walk the mare. She followed his commands on the cord bridle, and he stopped her often to fondle her as his brother had done. Finally he looked up.

"Bill," he called, "is it all right if I ride her? Is it? That'll show 'em like nothing else."

Mr. Boyer turned to Bill Dailey. "No one's been on her back in over a year. Don't let him. You'll be carrying your luck too far."

"Go ahead, Hank," Bill called to his brother. "Show 'em you can do what you want with her. Show 'em it takes only a little nerve an' a lot of kindness to win the respect an' confidence of most horses."

They saw the boy mount Wild Bess and ride from

one end of the barn to the other. After many minutes of watchful silence Mr. Boyer said, "I guess you must be the best horse-tamer in the world, Mr. Dailey."

"No, I'm not. I'm no better than you are. Just remember that you promised to handle her every day, an' to treat her kindly without lettin' her have her own way. That's where the trouble really started. You give this kind of mare an inch an' she'll walk away with you. But she'll respond quickly to kindness. So love her, love her *lots*."

Mr. Boyer chuckled. "Well, I don't know as I can go *that* far, Mr. Dailey, but I'll do my best, an' if I have any more trouble I know who to call. . . ."

A neighbor said, "Mr. Dailey, I got a horse that throws himself over backwards all the time. He's broken up two buggies and a wagon. If you can keep him on his feet, I'll gladly pay you *twenty-five dollars!*"

And another said, "I've got a kicker, Mr. Dailey—"

"Step right this way, gentlemen, and I'll make all the arrangements," Finn Caspersen interrupted eagerly. The big man's eyes were wondrously alive as if he had embraced a great cause and had visions of a world sorely in need of such a man as Bill Dailey.

Taming Secrets

4

Bill Dailey drove his bay mare home and tried not to listen to Finn Caspersen.

"It was a foolhardy thing you did, Bill, catching hold of her tail like that, but in all my days around shows I never saw anything more exciting!"

Bill said, "I guess I wouldn't do it again, but it worked out fine with Wild Bess."

Hank joined the conversation. "I'll bet it was the first time anyone ever thought of making a horse dizzy to win control," he told his brother.

"And I don't think anyone ever tried haltering a horse with a stick before, either," Finn added. "You sure made a mark for yourself today!"

Bill Dailey said nothing but he felt an excitement

stir within him that hadn't been there before his contest with Wild Bess. Maybe he *had* made an important discovery in the art of handling vicious horses. How could he put it to further use without risking his neck every time?

"I don't see why you won't be a professional horse-tamer, Bill," Finn persisted. "You're good at it. Better than you are at making carriages. And there's money in it, too."

"As I already told you, I'm no professional," Bill answered thoughtfully. "But if I could, I'd help a lot of people with their horses. Too many bad horses are the result of bad management. Jus' like Wild Bess was. More owners than horses need training." While his speech was clear and down-to-earth, his eyes were bright with a vision of launching a new kind of crusade, one through which both man and horse would benefit.

Finn said solemnly, "You could teach them. You sure could, Bill. And let me tell you how we'd go about it. Besides being a horse-tamer you'd be a lecturer. We'd have big classes and go around the county—"

"You'd make a road show of it," Bill interrupted. "I wouldn't want that."

"I wouldn't at all, Bill!" Finn protested. "We'd just try to reach as many people as we could. That's

what you want, isn't it? Doesn't it stand to reason
that if you hold big classes you'll be teaching more
people what you want them to know about horses?
Doesn't it, Bill?" Finn's eyes were bright with
excitement and his voice had the rhythmic cadence
of the professional showman. He had gained control
of his audience and his persuasive powers were
being brought into full play.

"Well . . ." Bill Dailey said undecidedly.

"Sure it does, Bill! First thing you know you'll be
the most sought-after man in the county, maybe
even the whole *country!* Where else are people
going to get the kind of help you can give them? Do
you know of any books written on the subject?
Think hard now. Any at all?"

"I know of one," Bill answered, "but I don't think
too much of it."

"I'd like to see it."

"It's home."

Upon reaching Birdsboro, Bill Dailey drove
through the town, carefully threading his way
around the many carriages and wagons that filled
Main Street. It was Saturday and the stores were
crowded.

"I'll bet there's not a person here who doesn't
have a horse with some bad fault that you could
correct," Finn said.

"Maybe so."

"And that's true of every town in the country. You'd be famous, Bill, maybe *world* famous!" he concluded expansively.

"You're crazy, Finn," Bill said, laughing. Having passed the busy grocery, hardware and drug stores he clucked to his mare and the carriage wheels spun faster over the dirt road.

"No, I'm not," the big man answered. "With me managing you you'd go far, Bill. Mark my words, you would."

"Don't listen to his wild talk," Hank warned his brother.

Finn Caspersen laughed recklessly. "You can be part of it, too, Hank. We'll use you like Bill did today. You'll close the show!"

"I told you I won't put on any *show*," Bill said quietly.

"I was just kidding."

"Then be serious if you want me to go in this with you. There'll be no more tail grabbin' like I did today, nothing so exciting as that. Instead it'll be just plain common sense, intelligent handling and kindness."

"No more tail grabbing?" Finn repeated disappointedly. "Is that what you said?"

"It's too dangerous an' I don't aim to get myself killed," Bill answered. "But I'm goin' to work it out some other way. Circling makes a horse match his strength against himself rather than against his handler. He gets dizzy and helpless without any pain or injury. It's an easy way to get control, to go on from there."

They passed the harness shop with its wooden, dapple-gray Percheron standing outside, then crossed the railroad tracks after listening for the whistle of the 12:09 from Pottstown. Just beyond was the stone courthouse with its park and bandstand in front. Next to that was the barnlike brick structure housing the jail, the town hall and the auditorium. It was there that Bill Dailey stopped to water his horse at a corner trough.

"Do you think Wild Bess will stay cured of biting?" Hank asked his brother.

"She will if Mr. Boyer keeps his promise. We'll go back in a couple of days to make sure."

Finn Caspersen looked at Bill with new respect in his eyes.

A few minutes later they were on their way again and, nearing home, turned down a well-shaded street with trim two-story residences set well back from the brick sidewalk and picket fences. Behind each house was a stable.

Bill Dailey turned into his driveway. Only the first floor of his house was different from the others on the street. It had been converted into a workshop and through the windows a multitude of carriage and wagon parts could be seen.

Arriving at the stable, Hank said, "Let me take care of her, will you, Bill?"

"You'll be sure to wash and rub her good?"

The boy nodded vigorously. "An' I'll walk her till she's dry."

"All right," Bill said, but already his thoughts were on other things. He hurried into the house, Finn Caspersen following closely behind.

They climbed a steep flight of stairs and entered the living room. "Have a seat," Bill said without stopping, "an' I'll get that book."

When he returned, Finn Caspersen had his coat and hat off and was sprawled in a deep leather chair. "Nice place you have here, and I'm making myself right at home," he said. "Hope you don't mind."

"No, I don't mind," Bill answered.

Finn picked up the book and thumbed the pages, finding it difficult to read in the room's dim light. The narrow windows, he thought, should be widened to let in more light and air. He decided that if he ever got around to owning a house he'd do a lot more besides widening windows. For one thing, he'd do away with dark, gloomy wallpaper such as this room had. In its place he'd put up a bright, cheerful pattern and he wouldn't care at all what people thought of him for doing it. He'd throw out all the heavy black-walnut furniture that was so popular as well as these horsehair-stuffed chairs and couches. He'd get something light and comfortable, that's what he'd do!

He glanced up from the book. "I can't see very well."

Bill Dailey hurriedly lit a gas lamp.

"That's better," and Finn smiled. "Thanks."

"This book's an old one belonging to my father," Bill said. "I couldn't find any others on horse management an' I've been trying everywhere."

"I'll bet you have," Finn mused while turning the pages.

"I don't think it's very good. There's nothing in it that'll help anybody in *real* trouble," Bill explained.

For several minutes Finn Caspersen read in silence, then he asked, "You mean something like this won't work?" He handed the open book to Bill Dailey and indicated the following paragraph:

Great Secret for Taming

Take one pound of oatmeal, a quarter pound of honey, half Lawrance and make into a cake and bake. Put the cake into your bosom and keep it there until it sweats. When the horse has fasted twelve or twenty-four hours give it to him to eat. Then use him kindly and gently.

"I'll bet we could sell a lot of those cakes, Bill,"
Finn suggested, smiling. "Read the next one too. I
like that even better."

Arabian Secret

To make a wild horse approachable or a vicious
horse gentle, take two parts of the oil of rhodium
and one each of cumin and anise. Put in a bottle
and cork tightly until ready for use. A little of
this is to be rubbed on the hands, and while held
before the horse approach from the windward
side. When near enough, rub a little on the nose
and in ten or twenty minutes the horse will be
ready to receive your kindness and plan of
teaching.

When Bill Dailey handed back the book, Finn
asked again, "Won't they work?"

"No better than apples or anything else that a
horse is fond of," Bill answered. "The only thing
that really works comes from here." He tapped his
head. Then, sternly, he said, "You're not figurin' on
turning us into a medicine show, are you? 'Cause if
you are . . ."

"No, no," the big man replied hastily. "I was just
asking, Bill. I didn't mean anything by it.

"Say, let me tell you about 'The Whisperer,'"
Caspersen went on, anxious to see a change in the
stern look on Bill's face. "This book kind of makes
me think of him. I knew him when I was a kid living
in Mallow in the County of Cork, Ireland. We
called him The Whisperer because he'd put his
mouth to a horse's ear as if he were whispering
something to him, and he had quite a local reputation for his power over horses. Some people even
thought his powers were supernatural."

Finn Caspersen stopped a moment and when he
continued there was more of an Irish lilt to his voice
than ever before. "Shure and I remember our
parish priest crossin' to the other side of the street,
he did, whenever The Whisperer came along! 'Tis
the truth I speak when I say he thought the man was
in league with the very divil himself!"

Finn laughed heartily and it was a few moments
before he turned again to Bill Dailey. All the
recklessness was back in his voice when he said,
"Now, Bill, I'm not suggesting for a minute that we
sell taming medicine, but where would be the harm
in whispering in a horse's ear? I heard you carrying
on quite a conversation with Wild Bess. It's great
showmanship."

Bill Dailey couldn't help smiling. "All right,
Finn," he said, "whispering once in a while won't

do any harm. But remember, we're going to play this straight or not at all. There's not going to be any trickery. Right?"

"No trickery," the big man agreed.

"No magic words," Bill went on.

"No magic words," Finn repeated.

"No taming medicines."

The big man shrugged his shoulders and repeated, "No taming medicines." His eyes met Bill's. "What do we have left?" he asked.

"Hard work."

"No nothing," Finn summed up, closing the book, "but I'm game to try it."

Thunder Rolls

5

Finn Caspersen stood on a box in front of the largest livery stable in Pottstown. He had rented the stable for Bill Dailey's first public appearance as a horse-tamer. Tacked on the doors were handbills which he had designed himself and had distributed about town. At the top was a drawing of Wild Bess with her teeth bared. The announcement read:

FOR ONE DAY ONLY

GREAT HORSE-TAMER OF THE WORLD, THE AUTHOR OF A NEW SYSTEM, PROFESSOR WILLIAM DAILEY, WHO RECENTLY TAMED THE WORST BITING HORSE IN THE COUNTY, MR. A. J. BOYER'S WILD BESS, WILL APPEAR AT THE MAIN ST. LIVERY STABLE, MONDAY, NINE A.M. SHARP.

The big man peered down at the crowd. "More than fifty of your friends and neighbors are already inside, folks, waiting for the Professor to begin his instruction in the world's best system of horse taming."

He stopped to wave away some boys who were trying to peek through the cracks in the closed doors.

"You will be astonished, my friends," he continued, "by the ease with which Professor Dailey subdues some of the most vicious and ungovernable specimens of the horse fraternity to be found in this vicinity. You will find both amusement and instruction in witnessing the skill with which he handles the hitherto incorrigible subjects brought forward to test his new doctrine. Before your very eyes he will subdue the wildest and most stubborn cases, attaining complete subjection and docility. Like Wild Bess, whom he tamed for Mr. Boyer just a week ago, they will be horses you know well from this *very* neighborhood. Yes, my friends, you will be astonished and astounded by the ease with which Professor Dailey brings them *all* under the control of Man! You will see him jump upon their backs, slide off and handle them without their showing the least disposition to bite or kick!"

Finn Caspersen paused, and a man called out, "For how much money?"

"For only five dollars, sir, truly a most reasonable fee for such combined entertainment and instruction!" He waved in the direction of his flat-bed wagon in which he had brought his most prized merchandise—several fine clocks, silver-handled buggy whips, rare books and guns.

"These are just a few of the valuable and *voluntary* gifts the Professor has received from grateful members of his classes," he lied. "I know there must be many among you who have difficult horses that you cannot manage and—"

A man interrupted defiantly, "My name is Clayton and I have such a horse but I do not care to join any horse-taming class. I can do as much with a horse as any man. I do not want instruction but I will gladly sell you the horse!" He laughed loudly and the crowd joined him.

Finn Caspersen waited soberly for the laughter to die down, then he said in his most courteous manner, "We do not want to buy your horse. But I'll tell you what we'll do, sir. If you join the class and bring your horse for Professor Dailey to experiment upon I promise that he will be gentled within twenty minutes!"

"Without hurting him?" the man asked disbelievingly.

"I guarantee Professor Dailey will not injure him the slightest bit."

The man was enjoying his role. "And what if your great horse-tamer doesn't gentle him in twenty minutes?"

Finn Caspersen smiled. He knew he had won over not only this man but the whole crowd as well. "If he doesn't, sir, I will charge you nothing for the instruction and will also buy you the best suit of clothes to be found in Pottstown!"

The crowd roared and the man shouted, "I will come on those conditions. I know that no man living can tame my horse within that time!"

From that moment on Finn Caspersen had no trouble selling the rest of his tickets.

The livery-stable ring was smaller than Bill Dailey would have liked it to be. Before him rose a high tier of seats filled to capacity, just as Finn had promised. The trouble was that if anything went wrong, someone might get hurt.

"I am no magician," Bill told the throng, his stern gaze sweeping the stands. "Neither am I a humbug as some of you might think." Tight-lipped, he paused a moment, waiting for a possible jeer. But no one challenged him. He knew what he had to say and he knew too that he would say it well, thanks to Finn's patient coaching.

"I seek only peace for the long-abused horses of our land," he went on. "Too many professional horsemen have kept what they know to themselves,

with some even pretending they have secret powers. There is no mystery to controlling horses. All it
takes is skillful, intelligent handling. When a horse
becomes vicious or unmanageable it is as the result
of ignorance and bad treatment. I propose to
educate owners as well as their horses, and to do so
without tricks or deceit. There are no secrets to my
system. It is based on these simple facts, which
anyone can learn.

"First, horses can be molded by firmness and
kindness. Second, because they have brains it is
possible to reach an understanding with them.
Third, it is not difficult to do this if you go about it
the right way. For example, if a horse's trouble is
caused by fear, you show him that there's no reason
to be afraid. If it's viciousness, which is far more
dangerous, you must rid him of it by kind but firm
treatment."

From the upper seats a man shouted, "Show us,
Professor, that's what we came for—*not a lecture!*"

The sternness remained in Bill Dailey's eyes as
he ignored the man's interruption. "I have challenged you to produce horses that you think I
cannot handle. They are here, waiting to be tamed.
In all frankness, what I am about to do here is
foreign to my real purpose, which is not to exhibit
feats of taming but to create more interest in the
fundamentals of control. If these horses had been

handled properly they would never have become vicious, ill-mannered and headstrong, dangerous not only to you and me but to men, women and children on our streets. They are capable of killing and maiming, causing destruction of life and property. They never should have been allowed to reach this condition and you *owners* are primarily at fault!"

The man to whom Finn Caspersen had promised a suit of clothes if Bill failed to tame his horse stood up and said loudly for all to hear, "Sir, I am one of those owners who await your education. Now, I do not consider myself a fool with horses. I have handled them all my life and can drive any common horse as well as the average man. I cannot see how it is possible by any reasonable treatment to control such a stallion as mine in the short time of twenty or thirty minutes which you claim to be able to do. It is contrary to all reason! I would be afraid to undertake to lead him into this ring without the aid of two good men for I doubt that we would be able to hold him. Why, he has never been harnessed or put in shafts in his life."

Pausing, the man turned to the others sitting around him. "I must warn you all that to experiment upon my horse in a crowded place such as this will not only be extremely difficult but exceedingly dangerous as well. The greatest care must be taken to guard against an accident resulting in serious harm to one or more of us." He sat down abruptly.

There was a smile on Bill Dailey's thin lips as he said, "There is no need to be afraid. I shall lead Mr. Clayton's horse before you without danger to yourselves. And I shall do it within twenty minutes. However, as I explained to Mr. Clayton a few minutes ago, there is much more to it. His horse Thunder will have to be treated at home according to my directions. I can do little more at this time than to make it possible for him to handle his horse and then prescribe further treatment. This applies to all of you whose horses I shall experiment upon. The after-treatment is most important in the management of every case, and I am at your call if you need help. Without the after-treatment your horses will not remain gentle. The methods I use may seem ludicrously simple to you. But they are in truth very beneficial and when properly applied will enable you, too, to continue effective control over your horses."

Turning away from the crowd, Bill Dailey went to the first stall where Mr. Clayton's chestnut stallion, Thunder, awaited him.

He was a large-boned horse, strong and compact. Bill estimated his age at about eight—an adult horse, strong-willed and capable of putting up the hardest kind of resistance. It had taken four men to bring him to the stables. Only a show of overpowering force would make any kind of an impression on Thunder.

Carrying his rope throwing rig, Bill spoke to the horse and entered the stall. Thunder was tied but nevertheless he lashed out with a hind leg. Bill worked quickly, his rope pliable from years of use. One loop with a large metal ring at the top went around the horse's girth. Another loop extended from it to the dock of the tail, acting as a crupper. Bill adjusted both loops to size and then tightened them. Next he took a strong cord from his pocket and fastened one end to the top of the girth loop, just above the metal ring. He carried the cord to Thunder's halter and then back through the metal ring, taking up slack. There was only one more thing left to do. He quickly picked up the horse's near forefoot and, using a short leather strap, buckled it to the girth loop. Now he had Thunder standing on only three legs.

"Now, *back* up," he said quietly but firmly, untying the horse.

As the stallion hopped backwards, his owner's voice shrilled, "I warn you, gentlemen! I warn you again to move up from all the lower seats. My horse cannot possibly be controlled by one man when he is free of his stall!"

The stallion lunged forward and Bill jumped aside

to avoid colliding with him. Then he tightened the cord quickly. Thunder's head was pulled around and his weight was thrown onto the same side as his disabled foot. He couldn't keep his balance and fell easily, rolling over on his side. Bill slackened the

cord and the stallion jumped up, lunging at him again. Bill hopped in a circle and pulled on the cord.

Down went Thunder once more, rolling over almost on his back this time. Bill slackened the cord and the stallion jumped to his feet.

Bill lost track of how many times he threw Thunder before the horse finally lay quiet with the cord slack. Bill went toward him then, his hands moving gently over Thunder's neck and head. For only a moment was there any resistance to his touch, then the giant muscles relaxed.

"Now get up, big fellow," Bill said softly, taking Thunder by the halter.

The stallion got to his feet and Bill continued stroking him. Finally he reached down and released the foot strap. Thunder stood quietly, and when Bill led him around the ring he was as gentle as a horse could be. The crowd watched in stunned silence.

After a few minutes Mr. Clayton rose to his feet. "You have worked some magic upon him!" he shouted.

"No, I used only common sense and a little skill which you, too, can learn," Bill answered. Mr. Clayton, defeated for the moment, sat down.

"We do not believe you!" another man called. "I know this horse well and I assisted Mr. Clayton in trying to gentle him many times. We used nearly thirty dollars' worth of heavy leather rigging on him and he kicked himself loose from all of it!"

Bill Dailey smiled. "My throwing rig can be made of any old rope in a few minutes' time and costs

practically nothing. It does the job and yet there's
no danger of hurting the horse. With it any man of
ordinary strength can throw the strongest horse as
quickly and as often as the animal gets up. Also, he
can hold him down or roll him back as he pleases.
The horse's resistance is thereby quickly broken. Its
effect is no different from that of a stripling throwing
a bully twice his size with ease—assuming some
skill on the stripling's part, of course. The bully
finally quits and stops being quarrelsome and
browbeating weaker people. I would now like to
explain how and when to use my rig," he concluded.

Mr. Clayton rose again, his face flushed with
anger. "Only medicine or something of that kind
could enable you to accomplish such a feat as this!"
He paused while the men around him nodded
encouragement. "Sir, we would like to smell your
hands and clothing."

For a moment Bill Dailey stood silently bewildered; then he said sadly, "Come along then, if that
is where we must begin. There is still much work to
be done."

Horse Magic

6

The next issue of the weekly Pottstown *Times* carried the following story:

Professor Wm. Dailey, the horse-tamer, has been in town the past week and has created a great stir among our horsemen. So great was the interest aroused by his first appearance that he was asked to remain longer. Prof. Dailey formed a school which was largely attended during the week by those interested in such matters, including many of our best citizens who have fine horses, and it seems to have been altogether satisfactory.

Indeed, it is the opinion of this writer that it is fortunate for Prof. Dailey that this is not an age when men are executed for witchcraft. Had he lived in Salem in 1692 and exhibited, as he has here, his power over refractory horses, he would have been hanged, as sure as fate, for a wizard. Actually, we are not certain that he does not practice some sort of witchery in his management of horses.

Mr. Roy Clayton's chestnut stallion, well known through the county for his viciousness, was first introduced and within a few minutes Prof. Dailey had him acting the part of a well-trained horse. Next came a spirited mare, whose stubbornness was not so readily but no less surely overcome. She was followed by an old stager, known locally as Betsy Lou, who for years had defied every blacksmith in the county. After five minutes' training by Prof. Dailey she stood quiet as a lamb while her feet were handled and hammered in true blacksmith style. There was another splendid horse whose principal fault seemed to be unusual fright at the sight of an umbrella. Within a very short space of time Prof. Dailey was able to move one of these articles before him and over his body without the horse showing the slightest fear of it. The last horse in the first day's exhibition was a puller on the bit who was beaten neatly at his own game and yielded handsomely, assuring Prof. Dailey of complete success for the day's work.

No one, however, can form an idea of his wonderful power over horses until he witnesses proof of it. To see a horse furious, stubborn, defiant, with the very devil in his eyes, calmed down by some mysterious power, rendered docile, patiently submissive and allowing every liberty to be taken with him, is hard to believe even though this marvelous transformation takes place before your very eyes!

Prof. Dailey has left Pottstown in order to fulfill numerous engagements throughout the county. We wish him continued success.

At home Bill Dailey threw down the newspaper. "It sounds as though you talked to this reporter," he told Finn Caspersen.

"Not at all. Had nothing to do with it."

"Then someone ought to tell him that there was no witchery to what I did in Pottstown. Those who attended my classes can now do what I did."

"I wouldn't say that," Finn replied quietly. "But they're better off than they were."

"So are their horses," Hank spoke up from a nearby couch.

"So are their horses," Finn repeated. "Say, Bill, now that you're a success and going on . . ."

"To Reading?" Bill asked. "Did you make the arrangements?"

Finn nodded his head. "The circulars are printed and up. I rented a bigger place this time, an old riding school." He ran a hand through his unruly hair. "You didn't whisper to the horses last week as you said you would occasionally. I was figuring that maybe in Reading . . ."

Bill Dailey left the table to get a drink of water. When he returned he said, "I'm goin' to be honest with people, Finn, and if you don't like it that way . . ."

"Aw, Bill, don't get sore now. I'm not asking you to be dishonest, just a little more of a *showman*. Give the people what they want, that's all. If you're going to talk to horses—and you do, you know— why can't you whisper to them once in a while? It's not going to do any harm and the people will love it. Besides, if they want to smell your hands and clothes, let them. Don't keep *insisting* there's no magic to what you do." He paused, his eyes holding Bill's. "There is, you know."

"You too?" Bill Dailey asked with bewilderment.

"Walking into that Clayton horse's stall and coming out alive was magic," Finn answered quietly. "He didn't *have* to get over as you told him to do. He could have kicked you into the stands before you got that rope rig on him."

Bill Dailey laughed and suddenly all the tension between the two men was gone. "That's not magic, Finn, that's *pretendin'*. When I looked him straight in the eye he had no idea how uneasy I was."

"You're not going to teach people things like that," Finn argued. "They either have it or they don't have it. So what I'm getting at is this: if they want to call what you do magic, let them. Don't just keep insisting it *isn't*."

"But that's exactly what I'm tryin' to accomplish," Bill explained again.

"You're trying to *reach* people," Finn corrected. "And unless you give them what they want you're not going to have an audience big enough to fill even a small livery stable. I know. I'm outside trying to get them inside. I know what they want. We ought to have a band and some trained ponies and horses to go along with us, too. You could show them how you drive without reins. We'd really pack them in, Bill. Just think of the number of people you'd be reaching and educating!"

Bill Dailey went to the kitchen window and looked out at the stable below. "If I did all that, you'd want to sell taming medicines next," he said, suddenly very tired. "You'd turn us into a medicine show."

"No, I wouldn't," Finn answered. "But even you said that the Arabian Secret stuff worked as well as apples or anything else a horse was fond of. The point I'm trying to make is that if people want to buy something more expensive than apples we might as well sell it to them."

"It's dishonest. If you start doing that, you'll end up selling—well, tincture of lobelia."

"What'll that do?" Finn asked curiously.

"Two ounces of it will make a vicious horse so sick he can't resist handling or anything else."

"Oh," Finn said. "A gypsy told me about something like that once. He said all you had to do to handle a bad horse was to boil a plug of tobacco in a gallon of ale and give it to him. What's wrong with that kind of taming?"

"The same as what's wrong with tying a horse down without food or water for days at a time, that's what!" Bill Dailey said sharply. "Any way you weaken a horse makes him gentle but when he recovers he's as bad as ever."

Bill Dailey sat down again, a tired look in his eyes. "But most important of all, such practices are cruel, Finn. I've known some of those medicines to cause severe colic and death. So if I ever catch you even thinkin' . . ."

"Now, Bill," Finn said uncomfortably. "I wasn't

thinking of anything but our show."

"It's not a show. It's a *class*. You've got to get that through your head, Finn. I'm aimin' to teach horse owners simple methods of control which will benefit both themselves and their horses. I want them to see that they can manage horses quietly and with no whipping or thrashing, no mauling or brawling."

"They'll still want to smell your clothes and hands," Finn said.

"I suppose so."

"They'll never think of you as anything but a showman."

"Some of them will," Bill said doggedly.

"They'll always want you to tame the most vicious, the worst-mannered horses in town. You'll risk your neck every time."

"I guess so."

"For peanuts," Finn pointed out.

"For peanuts," Bill repeated.

"My way we could play the biggest cities and fairs," Finn went on. "We could have our own canvas, large enough for hundreds, maybe thousands of people to watch. We'd put on a real show like Buffalo Bill does." Finn Caspersen shrugged his big shoulders. "Maybe I ought to go home and leave you alone. I got a hunch we'd both be better off."

"Go ahead, if that's the way you feel," Bill said.

Finn started to get up, then sat down again. "No, on second thought I'm going to stick around. Somewhere along the line you might change your mind about a lot of things, especially people. You haven't met as many as I have in my business. You'll get tired of having them smell your hands and clothes and asking to buy your *secret* taming medicines. Most people want everything made easy for them, even easier than the methods you'd like to teach them. When that time comes you'll start listening to me and that's when we'll start making money, Bill—real money, piles of it, more money than you ever dreamed of making in your life!"

Bill Dailey was smiling. "I don't dream about things like that," he said.

"You wouldn't," Finn said soberly, going to the door.

"Oh, Finn . . ."

"Yes, Bill?"

"I didn't tell you that I got a letter the other day from a Dr. Harrison, who heard we were comin' to Reading. He's got a tough horse named Tar Heel . . ."

"Did you tell him to bring him to us?"

"He can't. He's afraid to take him out of his stall."

"I get it," Finn said knowingly. "He wants you to stop off on your way."

Bill nodded.

"If you can't do anything with Tar Heel he's going to have him shot or something," Finn guessed.

Bill nodded again.

"And the doctor can't afford to pay you anything for your work."

Bill nodded, his eyes squinting in puzzlement. "How'd you know all that?" he asked.

"I didn't," Finn answered. "I just know *you*." The door closed behind his towering hulk as he left the room.

Tar Heel

7

Dr. Harrison lived in a two-story house next to a hospital and within easy reach of the center of Reading. He sat on a straight black-walnut chair and said, "It was very good of you to come, Professor, and I hope you'll be able to do something for my horse. No one else can."

"Is he a valuable horse?" Bill asked.

"As a foal he was looked upon as the most promising youngster in the state, being of the best trotting blood. Now I'm afraid he's known far and wide for his viciousness."

"When did it start?"

"At eighteen months he would look at a man pleasantly, yet bite, strike or kick as soon as he was within reach. He would fight as coolly and desperately as the very worst of brutes. If he could not reach a person with his forefeet or mouth, he would wheel and kick with the quickness of a mule."

"Yet you kept him."

"I had hopes of his changing as he grew older," the doctor answered.

"And did he?"

"No, I'm afraid he got worse, simply because no one could handle him. Many highly recommended horse-breakers tried and failed. Then I secured the services of Ralph Smith, one of our most successful and experienced local horsemen. He seemed to be getting along fairly well with Tar Heel until one morning, while Ralph was feeding him, the horse jumped for him, catching hold of his jacket and lifting him off the floor . . . and Mr. Smith weighs one hundred and eighty pounds."

Dr. Harrison's gaze shifted from Bill Dailey to the big man and the boy sitting on the couch. There was grave concern in his mild blue eyes.

"Mr. Smith was thrown to the floor of the stall," he went on, "and then Tar Heel actually *kneeled* on him. It was at that moment that I heard Mr. Smith's screams. A patient was visiting me and together we grabbed pitchforks and succeeded in getting the horse away from Mr. Smith before he could do further injury. Although all this happened six months ago, Mr. Smith is still under my care."

"Who's been taking care of Tar Heel since then?" Bill asked.

"I have. I've kept him shut up in his stall, waiting for such a man as you to come along. I cannot give him to anyone. I fear him and yet it is against my principles to have him destroyed. If you can subdue him, you will prove to me that you are the greatest horse-tamer in the world."

Dr. Harrison rose to his feet. "I'll take you to him now. The men you wanted here are waiting at the stable."

Bill Dailey stood up, his eyes puzzled. "Men? I asked for no men. Who are they?"

"Why, several of our most prominent citizens and a reporter from the newspaper," the doctor answered, his gaze shifting to Finn Caspersen. "Mr. Caspersen called yesterday and said . . ."

"I understand now," Bill said, turning and staring at the big man.

Finn shrugged his heavy shoulders, avoiding Bill's eyes. "Yes, Doctor, we'd like the people of Reading to know exactly how the Professor manages such a brute as yours. It is my hope that it will be fully reported in the newspaper."

"I'm sure it will," the doctor answered, leading

the way. "Everybody knows Tar Heel's reputation."

"Don't let me down," Finn told Bill as they left the room. "We could use this publicity."

A small group of men awaited them outside the stable. Dr. Harrison made the introductions but Bill Dailey's eyes were on a dog in the next yard; it had hold of its tail and was circling crazily.

A few minutes later Bill got his first look at Tar Heel. He was of the finest blood, as the doctor had said. He was coal black and light-boned, weighing not much over a thousand pounds. He moved about his box stall with all the grace of a panther, his head constantly turning toward the door. He was in every respect a model of flowing grace. But his eyes gave him away. They were snakelike. His forehead, too, was a little too low. Bill would have known without being told that here was a horse who would look pleasantly at a man one minute and strike the next.

Tar Heel was not too unlike Wild Bess, the main difference being that he had not been made vicious by incompetent handling or lack of care and kindness. No, Tar Heel had been born with a vicious quirk and would require careful management throughout his life. He was no horse for Dr. Harrison or for anyone else who was not an expert horseman. But that could be said later. Now . . .

Bill Dailey went to the stall door. The most

vicious horses were not always the most difficult to handle. If no one had tried cruel, old-fashioned methods on them, which was not the case here, they were very often the easiest to tame. But Tar Heel had been taught cunning and treachery to the highest degree by those who had attempted to manage him and failed.

Through the bars Bill watched the angry flashing of Tar Heel's eyes. The most dangerous thing of all would be what he had to do within the next few seconds. If he could reach the animal's side before Tar Heel turned upon him, he had a chance to go to work. The horse was wearing a halter and from it a lead rope still hung. How long had Tar Heel carried it? Since the day he had pulled it out of Ralph Smith's hands, seeking to maim and kill?

Opening the door, Bill spoke sharply. "Get around!" There was no outward evidence of his uneasiness. He knew that stallions above all other animals could sense strength or timidity in a man. If Tar Heel didn't yield to him in the next few seconds, the contest would be over before it had begun.

He looked straight into the stallion's eyes and saw the split second of indecision at his sharply spoken command. The moment had come and it took every bit of his courage to move forward. Softly, quickly, he crossed the straw to Tar Heel's side. He stood midway between the horse's head and hindquarters. If he had been too near Tar Heel's head the horse would have struck and bitten him. To have been too near the hindquarters would have given Tar Heel a chance to kick. Bill kept him undecided, unbalanced.

"Be still," he commanded firmly.

Those watching thought that the first thing Bill Dailey would do would be to reach for the halter. But he didn't. Instead, his right hand darted quickly from his side as he lowered his body slightly. When he had straightened he was holding the end of Tar Heel's long tail in his hands and, in a twinkling, had tied a knot in it. Tar Heel too was suddenly in action. The horse whirled around, reaching for the man with pointed head and bared teeth.

Bill kept close to Tar Heel, holding the long tail with one hand and reaching for the dangling halter rope with the other. He got hold of it and, bringing it back to the tail and through the hairs above the knot, tied it quickly. Then he jumped back. There was nothing more to be done just then. Tar Heel was tied to his own tail.

The rope was long enough to enable the horse to go around in a circle but not so short as to cause him to fall. Raging at the tug on his tail, Tar Heel went around faster and faster, like a pinwheel, while Bill Dailey watched and waited for him to expend his strength and energy. It would be easy after that. He wondered if the dog outside was still playing with its tail. The only difference between it and Tar Heel was that the stallion wasn't playing. He was fighting furiously without hurting anyone or himself.

As Finn Caspersen watched the spinning horse it seemed to him that they had the most exciting act in show business. He turned to the local people, glad he had invited them, especially the newspaperman. Leaning over, he told the reporter confidentially, as if all this had been foreseen, "And you might tell your readers, too, sir, that Professor Dailey will drive this black demon about the city for them to see the morning of our first exhibition at the old riding school. . . ."

The next day Tar Heel's taming was fully reported in glowing terms to the readers of the Reading *Tribune*, assuring Bill Dailey of a large audience when he opened on Monday.

Medicine Man

8

Monday morning Bill drove Tar Heel through Reading as Finn had committed him to doing. He hitched the black horse at Penn Square before a large crowd.

Finn stood by, noting with pleasure the looks of astonishment upon the spectators' faces. "Yes, ladies and gentlemen," he said, "this is the demon who was known to you only a few days ago as the most vicious horse of any age in the Reading area. Under Professor Dailey's skilled hands he has become as mild as a lamb. If we were to turn him loose he would wander about among you like an old truck horse!

"You can see that Professor Dailey has him under perfect control," Finn went on. "Note also that Tar

Heel will be driven without even so much as a strap
to keep the wagon from striking his heels. Yes,
ladies and gentlemen, the Professor has completely
gentled this wonderful horse, making him safe for
your crowded streets."

Finn got into the rear of the wagon where he had
Hank holding a large American flag. He waved his
stovepipe hat to the crowd and Bill took up the
reins, clucking to Tar Heel. It was in this spectacular manner that they drove through the main streets
of Reading.

During the week that followed, Bill made other
concessions to Finn's persistent demands for more
showmanship in conducting their classes. He was
willing to oblige so long as they were honest
demands. He bought Tar Heel from Dr. Harrison at
Finn's urging, knowing that the doctor could never
keep the black horse gentle anyway. He taught Tar
Heel to go without reins and drove him at the
beginning of each class. Up to a point, he admitted,
Finn was right. More and more people came to see
Tar Heel, and as a result he was able to help more of
them with their own horses.

At the end of his stay in Reading, the *Tribune*
carried the following story:

Professor Dailey's treatment of horses is entirely
new and reliable as well as humane and practical.

Without the use of club or any cruelty whatsoever
Professor Dailey is a worthy missionary bringing a
glorious reign of peace to the long-abused horses of
our land. His knowledge is indispensable, particularly to those who raise colts. He has given honest
study to his art. He regards the horse not as dull
and stupid but as an animal able to draw deductions
and to be molded by firmness and kindness. He
appeals to the understanding of his subjects,
endeavors to make an impression on the brain, and
to show cause for every effect. We honestly believe
he is the most skillful and successful horse-tamer
who has ever visited this city. We urge all residents
throughout the state to take advantage of Professor
Dailey's remarkable skill.

"We've done it," Finn said, putting down the
paper.

"Done what?" Bill wanted to know.

"Made ourselves famous, boy. Your services are
going to be in demand from now on!"

Finn was right. Bill Dailey's reputation for
handling fractious horses spread quickly throughout
the state and invitations to exhibit his skill came
from everywhere. The three traveled from town to
town, taming horses, educating owners and, even
though Bill charged only a small fee for his services
and sometimes nothing at all, making more money

than any of them had ever seen before.

Finn Caspersen bought a new suit. It was bottle green and had gilt buttons. With it he wore a yellow-striped waistcoat, a silk topper, white gloves and a flower in his buttonhole.

"It's just for the show," he said offhandedly.

Finn insisted, too, that they buy a new coach for their transportation from engagement to engagement. It was a Tallyho drawn by four white horses whom Bill taught to caper and rear at will. Seldom was so fashionable a sight seen outside New York City and people lined the roads to look in astonishment as Bill Dailey's sensational four-in-hand passed by. Only young Hank was unhappy, for Finn insisted that he sit high up on the back seat, waving a large American flag.

Their first big-city engagement was held in Pittsburgh, which had a population of more than a hundred thousand. Finn hired the largest carriage house in the city and went to work to fill it.

First he wrote the copy of the most sensational circular he had ever attempted. He proclaimed Professor William Dailey the "Greatest Horse-Tamer in the World," able to make any wild, unbroken colt so gentle within twenty minutes that he could be taken into the street and without bridle or halter ridden in any way the owner pleased! As an extra inducement, Finn Caspersen offered five

hundred dollars if Professor Dailey couldn't accomplish this remarkable feat!

He did not consult Bill about any of this, nor did he let Bill see the circulars before posting them all over Pittsburgh. He knew that his partner didn't like to make elaborate claims as to his ability, especially those that bordered on circus tricks and detracted from his serious objectives relating to horse management. On the other hand, he knew too that once the circulars were up Bill would be forced to go along with him. Besides, he had full confidence that they would not lose their five hundred dollars.

But what Finn did not take into consideration was the effect of blueberry pie on Bill Dailey's stomach. Bill felt squeamish just before he was due to go into the ring. "I shouldn't go on," he told Finn.

"But you've got to!" the big man insisted. "I've filled the place for you."

"Give them their money back."

"It's more than that. It's five hundred dollars extra I'll have to pay. It's just about all we've got saved. We'll be broke, *flat*."

"You were the one who wrote the circular," Bill pointed out.

"I didn't know what blueberry pie did to you. If you knew it made you sick, why'd you eat it?"

"I like it," Bill said simply.

"We'll have to sell our horses, coach, everything. . . ."

Bill rubbed his stomach. The cramps were gone. "I'll try it, Finn. If it gets worse, I'll have to . . ."

"Don't even say it," the big man said, pushing him into the ring.

The rented carriage house was filled to capacity. There were more people there than Bill had ever seen in one place in his life. He walked to the center of the ring, nervous and afraid, which did not make his stomach feel any better.

The huge crowd was waiting impatiently for him to begin. He said, "I know there is much interest in fine horses here, for your trotting races are among the best in the country. I-I therefore take it as a g-great pride and privilege to speak to you about the education of horses . . . and," he hesitated before adding, "their owners."

A man in the front row rose to his feet. "Sir," he said, "we are not interested in what you have to say about *our* need for education. Neither are we interested in the kind of circus tricks you have advertised. Riding a colt in the streets without use of bridle or halter is of no importance to us even though you may have a smart way of doing it. We are horsemen, sir, and there are those among us who have paid as much as $33,000 for a horse and would not sell him for $100,000! Our problems of horse management are *real* and we are not interested in learning *tricks!*"

Another man shouted, "Sit down, Mr. Lutz, and let the Professor say what he's got to say. It's him we came to listen to, not you. Besides, not all of us have high-priced driving horses. If he can fix me up with an easy way to drive my old Nell without her kickin' me to kingdom come I want to know it." He laughed heartily and the crowd joined in, relieving the tension.

As Bill Dailey laughed, too, his nervousness and fear left him.

"I'll do the best I can," he said. "I want to help everybody regardless of how much you've paid for your horses or what you use them for. Oftentimes your very life and property depend upon how much control you have over your horse. If he's vicious either by nature or from bad handling, he's dangerous and unfit for streets or racetrack. Something must be done to cure him. Most owners don't know how to go about it. They only make matters worse."

Another man in the audience stood up and shouted, "Don't try to pull the wool over our eyes by fancy talk, Professor. We've heard men like you before an' none of them have done us any good. You all want to keep any *secrets* you have to yourselves."

"On the contrary, sir," Bill Dailey answered

quickly. "There are no secrets to good horse management and I will tell you all I know. Furthermore, I expect you to teach my methods to others. In that way more men and horses will benefit than I can reach alone. I plan to go from town to town and from county to county throughout the country teaching my methods and soliciting the aid of my pupils in going forth in turn and helping others."

He stopped as a sharp stab of pain creased his stomach. It went away quickly and he continued. "What I have learned is, I believe, very important. It is worthy of your interest and study. I will teach you three methods by which you can control the most vicious and obstinate horses. They are simple in themselves but you must learn to use them with care and skill."

He stopped while another pain gripped his insides. It was several minutes before he could go on.

"You must learn which of my methods to use and this depends on the temperament of the horse. For example, if you should tell me what bad faults your horse has, I can, except in rare instances, tell you his color, size, the kind of head and general character he has. Then I select the best method suited to cure his faults. What has to be remembered is that what works on one horse may not work on another."

The cramps filled his stomach and once more he had to pause a long while before continuing.

"The horses I treat here in this ring will be brought under control within a very few minutes. Most of them, however, will not be completely cured. Only by repeating my treatment at home can success be assured. These horses then are merely for the purpose of exhibition—"

Someone shouted, "We've heard enough, Professor, and we think we know something about this matter of horse taming. Maybe we know more than you can tell us. Mr. Miller's got a horse here. Now if you can ride or drive him, as you say you can, you'll convince us that you can beat any man in the country at taming horses."

Bill Dailey answered, "Have the horse brought out then and I'll settle the matter very quickly."

A groom, followed by an elderly, well-dressed man who was apparently Mr. Miller, led a gray horse into the ring. The animal was as ugly as any horse Bill had ever seen, besides being large-boned and very strong. There was no doubt in Bill's mind that the horse would put up a furious fight regardless of all restraint. It would be a dangerous case to handle in a crowded building such as this, and yet he had no alternative but to go on. He watched the horse kick and jump, pulling on the long lead rope that his groom held expertly but cautiously.

Bill Dailey had started walking toward the horse when the attack of prolonged stomach cramps bent him double. He knew then that the matter of holding a contest with Mr. Miller's horse had been taken out of his hands. When he could straighten up everyone was looking at him expectantly. The huge arena was still except for the furious lashing of the gray horse's legs.

Bill faced the audience with great effort. "I am sorry but I cannot attempt to manage this horse now," he apologized. "I am sick and it would be very dangerous for all of us. Your money will be refunded. If you will come back tomorrow . . ."

There were loud hoots and catcalls from the crowd, and one man's voice rose above all others. "You thought you could pull the wool over our eyes, didn't you, Professor! No wonder you're sick. It's the sight of that there horse."

Bill Dailey's face turned pale, more from pain than from the harsh calls of criticism. "I'm sorry," he repeated.

The gray horse was rushing about the ring, jumping and kicking and altogether giving his groom plenty of trouble.

Hank was suddenly at his brother's side. "Don't listen to them, Bill. You did right. I'll get you to a doctor."

"No, you stay here with Finn. Make sure he returns their money, every penny of it."

After Bill Dailey had gone, Finn Caspersen took the center of the ring. "Now, gentlemen," he said in his most professional manner, holding his hands in the air, "there's no need to hurry. As the Professor said, your money will be returned. Please take your time." He paused, glanced toward the exit Bill Dailey had used, then cleared his throat and continued, "But for those of you who are interested in not returning to your unruly horses empty-handed, I have a few bottles of a taming medicine never before made available in this area. It's called Arabian Secret. All that's necessary for you to do, gentlemen, is to rub a little on your hands before approaching the animal . . ."

There were hoots of derision from many in the crowd but there were others who looked on interestedly. Someone shouted, "How much?"

"Only ten dollars, sir. A special price, if I may say so, due to the Professor's inability to perform. The usual price after one of our exhibitions is fifty dollars, but today we are reducing it to only ten. Step right this way, sir. . . ."

Humbug!

9

"I've no place in my work for a medicine man," Bill
Dailey told Finn the next day. He lay on a cot in a
far corner of the livery stable. Finn Caspersen sat in
a chair beside him.

"Just because I sold a few bottles of Arabian
Secret doesn't make me a medicine man or turn this
into a medicine show," Finn insisted.

Hank, who was sitting at the foot of his brother's
bed, said, "It wasn't a few bottles. I told Bill how
many you sold. It was close to a hundred."

The big man turned to the boy, his eyes glower-
ing.

"You stay out of this," Bill warned his brother.

Finn Caspersen got to his feet. "It's still only a
few bottles compared to what I could've sold if I'd

94

had more ready. If there were five hundred people in the building, there were another five hundred waiting outside." He grinned recklessly. "What are we arguing about anyway, Bill? At ten dollars a bottle we made more money than if you'd worked!"

Finn paused as if undecided whether to go on or not. His eyes found Bill's and he mistook what he saw there for indecision. Grabbing his chair, he moved it closer to the cot and sat down again. "Maybe this is the time I always said would come. Maybe it's time you listened to me for a change. I've put up with your high-minded ideas long enough."

From the bedside table he picked up the bottle of medicine which had been purchased at the drug store for Bill's upset stomach. "Do you think this is any better than what I sold today? No! It's a *cure-all*, a sure cure for everything and *nothing*. I've sold gallons of it in my day an' I'll be selling gallons more before I'm finished." Again he grinned. "Oh, this medicine isn't going to hurt you, Bill. Maybe it'll even soothe your upset stomach some. It'll help you about as much as our Arabian Secret soothes upset horses. So what's the difference if I sell one or the other?"

Bill Dailey sat up in bed but he didn't look at Finn. "You wouldn't stop even there," he said quietly. "I can see that now. It's not in you to stop. In addition to taming medicines, you'd soon be selling *cure-alls* for every injury and ailment horses have."

"But why not, Bill?" the big man asked seriously. "I'm sure you're as good a horse doctor as the next man, and better than most. There are close to twenty-seven million horses and mules in this country. Most people are treating their sick animals just the way their fathers told them. They'd listen to you just as well as to anyone else and they'd buy whatever you had to sell them!"

Bill refused to meet Finn's searching eyes. He knew the big man was right. Not much more was known about the care of sick horses than in ancient times, and barbarous methods of treatment were being used—hot and cold drenches, bleeding, turpentine and carbolic acid. Someday people would take more of an interest in veterinary work and the weird cupping machines and witch-doctor practices would be no more. The day might not be too far off, either; two private veterinary schools had opened in the East and another was being established in Chicago.

"Are you listening to me?" Finn asked.

"I'm listenin' to you."

"Then what about it? Nothing we sell will hurt anyone one bit and it might help some. If you're dead set against doing it during the show, we can sell the stuff on the street *after* your performance."

Bill turned to Finn. "How'd you like me to tame a wild zebra for our show too, Finn? That's what a circus man visiting Reading wanted me to do for his act with Barnum and Bailey. He said there's nothing in the world so hard to break and train."

"A zebra? A *wild* zebra? You serious, Bill? Do you really think you could do it?" Finn rose to his feet excitedly. "They say there's one at the New York Zoo that was captured in North Africa. Now you're talking, Bill! A zebra trained to drive would really pull in a crowd! We'll go to New York and set up a big arena. Along with a wild zebra we'll get the biggest horse we can find! Not only big but strong and ugly—the uglier the better—like that gray horse today. You can teach him to rear and kick and bite on signal. Next we'll get an iron muzzle for him."

"A muzzle?" Bill asked curiously. "What's that for?"

"For him to wear, of course," Finn answered. "I want him to be as celebrated for his viciousness as you will be for taming him."

"And I'm to tame him over and over again?" Bill asked.

"That's right—at every performance. It'll be the most exciting exhibition in New York. Later on we'll travel to other big cities. Maybe even go to Europe! Think of that, Bill!"

"I am thinking of it," Bill Dailey answered. "It would be a circus, all right."

For the first time Finn became suspicious. "Are you *really* being serious?" he asked.

"Sure," Bill said steadily, meeting the other's searching gaze. "About as serious as I am in training a wild zebra to be driven." He paused for only a second, his eyes as cold as his voice. "We're through, Finn. Get out and stay away from me."

The big man said nothing for several minutes. He might have been strong enough to pick up Bill Dailey with one hand and drop him to the floor, but he didn't try. Instead he recalled the day they had met when he had been whipping his gray colt. The same look was now in Bill Dailey's eyes and there was latent power in the slight figure that lay quietly beneath the blanket. Finn Caspersen decided, as he had then, that it would be better not to tangle with this man.

"Sure I'll go, if that's the way you want it," he said finally. "Maybe it's best for both of us, as I said some weeks ago. But I'm not going back to peddling merchandise, Bill. You gave me an idea today, a good one."

Finn rose to his full height, towering over the cot. "Remember how you told the folks that you wanted them to learn what you know and then go out on their own, teaching others? Well, that's what I'm going to do, Bill. Who knows your methods better than I do?" He grinned. "Of course, I'll add my own stuff. I'll play it big, bigger than you ever dreamed! I'll be the most famous horse-tamer in the world *and the richest!*"

Bill Dailey looked at him with contempt. "You have no sense of responsibility, Finn, an' that's what my methods require as much as skill. You're a fraud and you'll take advantage of a horse and his owner to achieve your dishonest goals." He got out of bed and stood unsteadily on his feet. "If I hear of you exploiting people and hurting horses, I'll come after you. Mark my words, I'll track you down an' expose you for what you are!"

Finn Caspersen shifted his ponderous weight from one foot to the other. Why should a slight man like this put him on the defensive? Furious with himself, he turned away abruptly. "Don't get so excited, Little Atlas," he said with attempted humor. "You're going to get your stomach all upset again. And remember, while I'm gone no more blueberry pie!"

He strode from the building as if he knew exactly where he was going and what he intended to do.

The next day Bill Dailey visited the owner of the gray horse. If he could get Mr. Miller to give him another chance, other serious-minded horsemen would come to watch his exhibition. But he met with flat refusal.

"You are a humbug," the elderly man said, shaking his bald head. "We can learn nothing from you."

Bill stood uncomfortably before the large office desk. "I can prove to you that I was really sick. I have a note from Dr. Patt."

"Oh, I don't doubt that you were sick," Mr. Miller answered, his eyes on the papers in front of him. "But you sold ninety-seven bottles of your taming medicine at ten dollars a bottle. That means you fleeced our citizens of nine hundred and seventy dollars."

"It was my manager who did it, not I. He's gone. There won't be any more sold."

The man shrugged his thin shoulders. "I don't mean to tell you your business and, I suppose, you can sell as much of your medicine as you like if people want to buy it. I simply refuse to have any part in such transactions.

"B-But it's not what I wanted at all," Bill persisted.

The old man looked up from his desk. "We were led to believe it *wasn't*, by your reputation. We had looked forward to—"

"Then why don't you give me another chance,

Mr. Miller?" Bill pleaded. "I have never deceived people and pocketed their money. I'll even open up the doors and let everyone in free for this first class!"

"So you might sell more bottles of your Arabian Secret?"

"Of course not!" Bill pounded furiously on the flat desk. "Can't you understand that I mean every word I say? I want you and your gray horse back *so I can prove the value of my system*."

Without answering, the old man studied Bill Dailey's face. Then he turned back to the papers on his desk and shuffled them nervously.

"Will you do it, Mr. Miller? Will you?"

"I know my gray horse very well," the old man answered gravely. "You cannot manage him."

"At least give me a chance to try."

"Is he the only case you'd have to exhibit?"

Bill nodded. "All the other horses were removed by their owners. It won't be the first time I've been limited to a particularly bad horse to manage. It won't be the last."

"No, I guess it won't," the old man said, looking up from his desk. "And you don't like it at all, do you?"

"No," Bill admitted. "Cases like that don't prove the true value of my system. People who watch me work so hard on extremely bad horses think it would be just as difficult handling an *average* horse, and it wouldn't be at all."

Mr. Miller smiled for the first time. "But I don't suppose bad horses hurt your reputation any."

"No, they don't. But that kind of publicity isn't what I'm after."

The old man rose to his feet, extending his hand. "I'm afraid I can't help you, Professor. I'm sorry. You see, my horse . . ."

Bill felt the sudden rise of anger within him. He sought to quell it by saying quietly, "I know your horse is worthless but I'll give you five hundred dollars for him."

The smile left Mr. Miller's face and his hand dropped to his side. "You'd pay that much money just to get him in the ring with you?"

Bill nodded.

The old man said, "You're right, of course, in saying that he's worthless. It's ridiculous for you to pay five hundred dollars for the opportunity of exhibiting your methods upon him. You cannot possibly succeed. No one could."

Bill ignored the man's challenge. He took five hundred dollars from his wallet, all the money he had left in the world, and placed it on the desk. "Will you sell him to me?"

Mr. Miller nodded and Bill Dailey left the room. He had made the worst purchase of his life. But he had done it for the chance to demonstrate that there were no secrets to good horse management . . . while Finn Caspersen had left town with $970 with the aim of showing that there were.

The Mustang

10

Mr. Miller's gray horse was known throughout the Pittsburgh area as the Mustang. He had been shipped from the West with a carload of wild horses, and although he possessed great powers of endurance and strength there was nothing well-bred about him.

The Mustang was as ugly as Tar Heel had been handsome. Bill Dailey watched him being led into the ring for the second time, realizing more than ever that he'd thrown his money away in buying him. Worse still, and more important, he began to doubt his ability to control such an animal before the large crowd that had returned to watch. If he failed, he'd be worse off than before and penniless as well.

He took the Mustang from the groom and held him by a long lead rope. Unlike his first appearance in the ring, the Mustang was quiet, much too quiet. He crouched near the rail, never raising a hoof and apparently indifferent to the noise and gazes of the spectators. There was something about his appearance that bothered Bill Dailey. He had never seen another horse like this one.

The Mustang had his head down and his ears, which were as heavy and long as a mule's, were thrown back and outward. His underlip was large and it hung down, leaving his mouth partly open. His eyes were sullen, those of a wild animal, and his nostrils were huge. He was long-haired and at present very dirty, probably as a result of not having been groomed in many months. But outlined beneath his unkempt coat was a body of heavy bone and muscle.

He was the worst horse Bill Dailey had ever seen *and the most dangerous*. There was no telling what the Mustang would do.

The crowd was more quiet now, waiting for Bill to start. He glanced at his young brother, nodding and trying to reassure him that this horse was no different from any of the others he had tamed. But he saw that Hank wasn't being fooled.

"Let me have my stick," Bill called to him.

He turned back to the horse, speaking to him

kindly, but his voice had no effect on the sullen eyes or the hanging head. Bill touched him lightly with the long slender stick Hank had given him, to learn what the Mustang would do when prodded and under pressure. He found out immediately.

There was a quick unwinding of the crouched body as the horse jumped and struck out furiously with both fore and hind legs. But his flaying hoofs were wide of their mark, and he stopped almost as soon as he'd started. Once more he crouched by the rail, his eyes rolling now and his huge nostrils opening and closing like a bellows.

As Bill watched him, he knew for certain that taming this horse would take days and days of work and that even then . . . He listened to the murmurs from the crowd that was waiting for him to go on. He started forward.

Strangely enough, the Mustang made no move as he approached him. Bill got close enough to touch the shaggy body with his hand; the horse continued standing quietly and sullenly.

Bill got over his surprise quickly. He was ready for anything, for now he knew that it was the nature of this horse to strike when apparently submitting to control. His resistance followed no set pattern. He was unpredictable and therefore extremely dangerous.

Bill picked up the shaggy tail and knotted the

end. The gray horse remained still. Bill put the halter rope through the tail and tied it with a half-hitch knot so he'd be able to release it quickly when necessary. There was still no resistance on the part of the Mustang, only a more noticeable blowing of his nostrils.

Next, Bill attempted to pull the horse in a circle, but the Mustang wouldn't budge. Even being prodded with the stick had no effect on him. As Bill prodded harder the Mustang dropped to his side and lay quietly.

There was nothing left to do but untie the tail. As soon as Bill did so, the Mustang jumped to his feet and came at him with battering hoofs which he narrowly avoided. But this was the kind of resistance Bill was used to and knew how to handle. He moved to the horse's off side and took the long, thin cord from his pants pocket.

The Mustang quit resisting control as suddenly as he had begun. Once more he crouched, his eyes rolling, his mouth drooping. Once more he awaited his chance to strike.

Bill put the cord around the horse's neck, adjusting it to size as he had done with Wild Bess so many weeks before. But this bridle would not be as simple as hers had been. More than guidance was needed here. Bill whipped the cord around the Mustang's head and as the horse reached for him with gaping mouth he pulled the cord through it. Once more he put the cord around the head and now he was able to exert bridle pressure on the Mustang. He pulled the cord slightly, forcing the horse's mouth open and drawing the cord through it again.

Suddenly the Mustang struck out, fighting control. Encouraged, Bill drew back on the cord again. The success of all his methods lay in overpowering resistance within a short time. Only if the Mustang fought the bridle and was quickly overpowered by its force was there any chance of achieving control over him.

As he worked, Bill kept watching the horse's eyes for they would tell him how far he should go. He wound the cord around the head once more, careful not to pull too tight and to exert pressure only when necessary. This cord bridle was safe and reliable but it had to be used with great care and judgment. It applied pressure to a horse's most vulnerable spot, a point behind the ears. The more cord that was used, the greater the pressure, and it could not be left on too long or the horse's life would be endangered. Bill used it only when he had to and in this case it was absolutely necessary.

And all the while he never let his attention be drawn away from the Mustang's eyes. They did not soften. The horse fought the bridle silently. He

bore the pressure without striking out. After fifteen minutes Bill Dailey knew the horse had won. To keep applying pressure would not only be unrewarding but dangerous as well. He unwound the cord from the horse's head.

As soon as the pressure lessened, the Mustang struck out again, this time catching Bill a glancing blow on the leg. The man fell back, twisting his body and rolling under the horse to avoid its hoofs. Then he leaped to his feet, catching hold of the halter again. The Mustang stopped fighting immediately, his huge nostrils opening and closing like wind-driven shutters. Once more he waited cunningly.

Bill had only one method left to try and that was to throw the Mustang repeatedly. He had little confidence that this would prove successful. Disabling the Mustang wholly or partly seemed to have little effect upon him, and throwing him would not be apt to create in him any more of a sense of helplessness. He would simply wait, as he was doing now, for another opportunity to strike out again.

Bill called to his brother for his rope throwing rig. He had no trouble putting it on the Mustang and drew it tightly over his back and around his tail.

Only when Bill tied up his forefoot did the Mustang make an attempt to break away. He hopped backward, trying to bite.

Bill let him go. He had the rope rig on and the slack taken up. He could throw the Mustang at will. He waited for him to stop hopping and noted again the wild look in the rolling eyes. All at once the horse came to a sudden stop. Before Bill could throw him he dropped down of his own accord and lay sullenly in the tanbark of the ring.

There was loud laughter from the crowd, and Bill knew only too well that he had to admit defeat. He could do nothing more here. Outdoors he would have had a better chance. If he worked on the Mustang day after day, he might eventually win control. But even then he wasn't sure. He doubted that the Mustang would ever be completely tamed.

Luckily, there were few horses like him.

Suddenly the Mustang jumped to his feet and before Bill could pull him down again, the air was split by a furious onslaught of hoofs. Bill dropped to the ground and pulled the cord hard, upsetting the horse and toppling him over.

Then Bill got to his feet and without taking his eyes from the Mustang said, "Gentlemen, this horse cannot be broken before a class. No one in the world could do it in such a short time. Give me a week and I'll drive him between shafts for you in this very ring. But he'll never be truly safe on city streets."

This had been his first failure before a class but he knew it wouldn't be his last. There would be other Mustangs in the years to come.

From far back in the crowd some men were jeering him, and Bill's face flamed with anger.

"If you've learned nothing else today," he shouted, "I hope you at least understand that it's wise to stop taming when either you or your horse becomes too excited."

"You're the one who's excited, not the Mustang!" a man answered, laughing.

"I hope you'll return with *average* cases," Bill replied. He had nothing more to say. He waited for them to leave.

Suddenly he heard an old man's voice which was familiar to him.

"Gentlemen, I'm afraid my friends and I have played a very bad trick on Professor Dailey," Mr. Miller told the crowd as he got to his feet. "We have known for a long time that the Mustang is completely unmanageable unless the most brutal methods are used on him. We have been most impressed by the Professor's attempts to handle him and I for one wish now to apologize and vote him a round of thanks for coming to our city. I have here the five hundred dollars that he paid for my worthless horse and will return it immediately. Mr. Haines, on my right, has a horse outside who is deathly afraid of trains and he would like Professor Dailey's help. Mr. Gordon here has a horse who balks and Mr. Smith has one who's afraid of dogs. . . ."

Bill Dailey listened to the high, nasal twang of Mr. Miller's voice and thought it the sweetest, most satisfying sound in the whole wide world.

On the Road

11

At the end of the week the Pittsburgh *News* carried the following story:

A NEW ART BY PROF. DAILEY

True to his word, Prof. Wm. Dailey drove Mr. Miller's vicious brute known as the Mustang between shafts about the ring of the Carlton Street Carriage House, where the famous horse-tamer has been conducting classes all week. In his last session here Prof. Dailey exhibited his skills before a throng such as has never been seen before in Pittsburgh. The people who filled the arena to the very rafters were attracted by that natural morbidity of the human mind which expects to be gratified by seeing some appalling disaster. In this case they were most grievously disappointed for instead of seeing the Mustang "mash things," as was his wont, they saw a docile animal driven by a gentleman who appeared neither alarmed nor expectant of any serious results from driving such a horse. At the close of his exhibit Prof. Dailey stated that although he has succeeded in taming and driving this vicious brute he did not feel that the Mustang would ever be safe on city streets. He has made arrangements for Mr. Miller to send him back west.

It is with deep regret that the horsemen of Pittsburgh bid good-bye to Prof. Dailey for they have acclaimed his system of educating horses and unanimously and enthusiastically endorse him and his methods to the public at large. His success here has been unprecedented and his teachings unparalleled in their field. What the members of his classes have learned could not be bought elsewhere for ten times the sum paid for the instruction. Prof. Dailey goes to Butler from here and we bespeak for him a hearty welcome there and the usual success attending his efforts. The Professor is a man of his word, professing no more than he performs, and doing good wherever he goes. In his teachings he not only instructs his scholars but also benefits the horses by introducing a more humane and gentle course of treatment, and therefore merits the name of benefactor to the brute race. We congratulate the people of Butler on their acquisition!

In Butler, Bill Dailey worked under canvas for the first time. The annual fair was being held there and he was asked to exhibit his skill. At first he did not like it at all. The slick shell-game operators and carnival men reminded him too much of Finn Caspersen. Whenever he looked at a sideshow poster or listened to a spieler claiming whatever was inside to be *"The most reemarkable on the face of the earth!"* he could not help thinking of Finn. To make matters worse, the grounds were filled with medicine men selling their Indian cure-alls for every ailment a person might have.

When he went to work in his big tent he found that he soon forgot Finn Caspersen. Never before had he met so many serious horsemen. The majority were farmers, there to enter sleek teams of horses, fat oxen, pigs and fine cattle in the fair competition while their wives displayed canned fruits, quilts and needlework. Such men were eager to learn all Bill could teach them about handling horses and he worked harder than he ever had in his life. By the end of the week he had made many more friends.

From Butler he went to Johnstown, Altoona and Williamsport, where he had no trouble filling his classes to capacity. His reputation as a horse-tamer and educator was spreading quickly throughout the East. The Williamsport *Mirror* informed its readers of this fact.

PROF. DAILEY WITHOUT RIVAL

During the present week Prof. Dailey, the celebrated horse-tamer and educator, has conducted his classes in this city. He has created a genuine furor among all interested in horses, and his reputation has extended to a large section of the countryside, for people have attended his classes from over twenty miles distant.

Prof. Dailey has succeeded in subduing and rendering perfectly tractable horses that have resisted all previous efforts of horse-breakers and others to reduce them to submission. His wonderful power over horses excites the most astonishment from those who are the best posted in equine care and treatment. The exhibition of his skill in driving trained horses without the use of bridle or reins is superior in interest to the choicest feature of the best traveling circus today.

Bill Dailey put down the newspaper and turned to his brother. "I wish they wouldn't keep comparing us to a travelin' circus," he said.

"What difference does it make as long as they come to see you?" Hank asked. "The more people you reach, the better job you do."

Bill grinned. "You're startin' to talk like Finn. I wonder where he is?"

"I thought we weren't to mention his name again," Hank said in surprise.

"I'm gettin' over him. I'd like to know what he's doin'."

Bill soon found out. He had finished his last class in Williamsport and was getting ready to move on to his next engagement in Scranton when he was handed a circular by a member of his class who asked, "Do you know this fellow?"

The circular read:

BOSS HORSE-TAMER
OF THE WORLD,
AUTHOR OF A NEW SYSTEM!

PROF. FINN CASPERSEN
EXHIBITS DAILY AT
NEW YORK AMPHITHEATER

Bill Dailey said quietly, "I know him, all right. He's a charlatan, a humbug."

A look of surprise came over the man's face.

"You'd have a hard time convincing his audiences of that fact," he said. "I have just returned from New York and this man has gained a very wide reputation for himself."

"His only experience with horses is driving one behind a peddler's cart!" Bill exploded with mounting anger. "Did you see him exhibit?"

"No, but my friends did, and they were very much impressed by him."

"He'll seriously injure or kill horses if he isn't stopped," Bill said with grave concern.

The man smiled. "I believe you're unduly upset, Professor. After all, New York is the greatest metropolis in the country. Its horsemen are among the most skillful and critical in the world, I imagine. They wouldn't be easily fooled, and this man Caspersen has certainly won their attention."

"He knows enough about my system to interest them," Bill answered, "but he never took the time to learn it well. Nor does he have the sense of responsibility or patience to do so."

Again the man smiled. "You sound almost jealous of your friend's success, sir."

"He's no friend of mine," Bill replied abruptly. "If he's subduing horses before an audience, I know exactly how he's getting away with it."

"I'm told he whispers in their ears and rubs

something on their noses. It seems to work like magic."

"He should be stopped," Bill said, more to himself than to his visitor.

"He also seems to be something of a horse doctor," the man went on. "He has excellent remedies for the cure of spavin, ring-bone and other diseases of horses."

Bill Dailey shook his head in bewilderment. "And yet you say New York horsemen are among the most critical in the world?"

"In my opinion they are," the man answered.

"I think you're wrong if Finn Caspersen is sellin' them his taming medicine and cure-alls."

The man resented Bill Dailey's criticism and there was sarcasm in his voice when he challenged, "Since you're so convinced Caspersen's a fraud why don't you expose him?"

"I will," Bill said, "right after Scranton. I'm not goin' to break faith with those people. When I'm through there, I'll go to New York and find Finn Caspersen."

Steaming Demon

12

Locating Finn Caspersen in New York City was not a simple task, as Bill learned upon his arrival. It was his first visit to the huge metropolis and its activity overwhelmed him. Hank too was bewildered.

As they passed through the streets early one Sunday afternoon no one paid the least bit of attention to Bill's skill in driving four-in-hand, much less to his coach which he had thought the handsomest in the land. After all, he was only one in a parade of many horses and carriages much finer than his own, some of which were also being driven four-in-hand. Bill noted too that the drivers all wore silk toppers, striped waistcoats and boutonnieres, and that sitting beside them were the most fashionably dressed and beautiful women he had ever seen in his life.

"I never saw so many howling swells!" he told his brother, awe in his voice.

"And, I doubt, better horses," Hank said in the same awed voice. "There's nothing big, fat and slow about these. They're lookers, all of them."

"So are the girls," Bill added. "It seems that we're doin' the fashionable thing on a Sunday, Hank."

They found the city itself as forbidding as it was strange, for the streets were crammed with block after block of houses and buildings. Yet they admitted to each other that they felt the strong pull of New York. Here was violent power and excitement! It was a city that would be forever on the rise and constantly changing. They wondered if this in some way was not beauty in itself.

They stopped in astonishment when they came to a railroad built in the air on towering iron trestles. Cars rattled past, drawn by a steam engine belching sparks and smoke. Their horses screamed and Bill had all he could do to quiet them as ashes, water and oil splattered on them from above. Other horses besides their own were frightened but what was most surprising was that many weren't! It proved that horses could get used to *anything*.

Hank watched the elevated train in dread, fearful that it would jump the tracks and tumble to the street below. Its speed must have been well over thirty miles an hour! No one would ever get *him* to ride in such a contraption, never in his whole life!

Bill turned his horses away from the sight, and not until he was several blocks from the elevated railroad did he slow them to a walk. His gaze strayed often to the horse-drawn cars on the tracks in the middle of the streets and he wondered how long such street cars could compete with the steaming demon they had seen a few moments ago.

Upon reaching the East River they stopped to watch the traffic passing over the brand-new Brooklyn Bridge. High above the water it hung from curved cables swung between two gigantic towers on opposite shores. To see this a few minutes after seeing the elevated train was almost too much for one day! Finally they turned away, wondering more than ever how they would be able to find the one man they were seeking in so big a city.

When they went across town again they came to a thoroughfare called Broadway. There they found luxurious hotels and theaters. The sidewalks were jammed with people, and there was no letup in the carriage traffic. It took all of Bill's skill to avoid accidents and at the same time observe everything that was taking place on both sides of the fabulous avenue.

He noted the lavish facades of the theaters with the strange new bulbs which Mr. Edison had invented. "Incandescent" they were called and he wondered if they would ever replace gas-lit lamps.

An actress named Lillie Langtry from London was beginning an American tour, he learned from a large poster. He passed the Casino Theater, which interested him very much because of a group called the Casino Girls whose pictures were outside this luxurious temple of beauty. He stopped the horses to read the name below the picture of the blond actress—Lillian Russell. It would be nice to meet her, all right.

Farther on they passed the new Metropolitan Opera House and then turned east, going back to Fifth Avenue. At 59th Street they came to the southern boundary of Central Park and felt more at home at once. Eagerly Bill drove his horses into the wooded area. The carriage roads were perfect and there were miles of bridle trails alongside. Many women were riding horseback and this surprised Bill and Hank very much, for such a thing was never done in Pennsylvania.

They found out, too, that here in the park the carriage parade was the most fashionable and exciting of all. They saw elegant victorias carrying

ladies even more elegant than those they had seen before, with tiny parasols delicately poised over their heads. They saw barouches, roomier and more stately than the victorias. Light, swift phaetons were to be seen, too, some even driven by young ladies with grooms stolidly perched on the back seat to help in case of trouble. There were dog carts as well. Bill had built many of these but had never liked them because of the back-to-back seating arrangement. And always part of the scene were the carriages of the conservative elderly dowagers taking the air in Central Park. These women remained concealed in stately broughams, their

coachmen and footmen soberly liveried, and their
horses always huge, fat and slow.

Never had Bill Dailey been so impressed as by
this passing scene. But the greatest shock of all
came when a woman went by, sitting on the box
seat of a coach like his own and skillfully driving four
horses.

"Now I've seen everything!" he told Hank.

"No, you haven't," his brother answered. "Look
what's coming up behind us."

Bill Dailey turned just in time to see several
horses whip by, each pulling a light two-wheeled
sulky. There was nothing showy about these horses.

They were bred and built for speed and endurance. Their bodies were long, lanky and bony and their legs moved with pistonlike precision in a remarkably fast trot. They disappeared quickly up the path, their drivers sitting motionless with the reins in their hands.

"Racehorses," Bill explained, "on their way to Harlem Lane, I suppose. I was told it's at the other end of Central Park. They've got the world's fastest trotter up there. Goes a mile in two minutes seventeen and a half seconds."

"No!" Hank gasped. "That's flying!"

"It's fashionable to own fast horses now, though it wasn't years ago," Bill said.

"Y'mean fast horses are no longer a sign of a fast man?"

"That's right," and Bill grinned.

When they left the park Bill stopped the carriage and, leaning out, asked a man on the street, "Sir, can you tell me where to find Finn Caspersen?"

"Finn what?"

"Finn Caspersen," Bill said loudly.

"What's that?" the stranger wanted to know.

"It's the name of a man I'm trying to find. He's appearing in an amphi-amph . . . a big arena here."

"Never heard of him."

Bill Dailey clucked to his horses. "Thanks,

anyway," he said.

"Say there!" someone called. "You looking for Finn Caspersen? Is that the name you just asked for?"

A man in a rakish phaeton behind a pair of sparkling bays pulled up alongside. "Yes," Bill Dailey said eagerly. "Do you know him?"

"The Boss Horse-Tamer? Is that the one?"

Bill Dailey did not reply. He could not bring himself to accept this description of Finn. Hank nodded for him.

The man went on, "You're too late. You won't find him here."

"Oh," Bill said, certain that the New York City horsemen had run Finn Caspersen out of town.

"He's in Europe," the man went on. "Got an invitation to tame a horse before the Queen of England! He's good, he is! Sailed over a week ago. Too bad you missed him. He puts on a show that's worth seeing."

The man paused, startled by the stunned look on Bill Dailey's face. "You don't have to look so disappointed as all that, mister. He'll be back soon, the papers say. Maybe you can find out the date by going over to the Fifty-ninth Street Amphitheater. His stable manager's there. You can't miss the place. Just keep going across town and you'll run right into it."

Bill Dailey picked up his reins. "Thank you," he said quietly. "Thank you very much."

"Don't mention it. I know how you feel. It's magic what he does with horses, something to see!"

After a few minutes' driving Hank asked his brother, "How do you account for his success here, Bill? They seem to be good horsemen."

"Fine horses and carriages don't necessarily make fine horsemen, an' if New Yorkers have accepted Finn on the little he knows about horse management, I'm stickin' around myself."

The 59th Street Amphitheater was the largest building in which Bill and Hank had ever found themselves. The ring was several hundred feet in diameter and towering above it was tier after tier of wooden seats. The stable to the rear held many stalls, most of which were occupied.

They had no trouble finding Finn Caspersen's manager, for his particular section of the stable carried a large poster over the corridor.

FINN CASPERSEN'S STABLE
BOSS HORSE-TAMER
OF THE WORLD

"Are all these horses Mr. Caspersen's?" Bill Dailey asked. The stable manager had Finn's height and heft. There was no doubt in Bill's mind that between the two of them they would be formidable opposition for almost any horse, especially if they were not particular as to the methods they used.

"Some of 'em," the man replied cagily in answer to the question. "Some belong to his clients."

"Clients?" Bill repeated.

"People he's tamin' 'em for."

"Oh."

"You a friend of Mr. Caspersen's?"

"We've worked together," Bill admitted.

"Horse-tamin'?"

Bill Dailey nodded.

"What's your name?" the stable manager asked.

"Dailey . . . Bill Dailey."

"Oh, yeah. I've heard him mention workin' with you. Guess you know what this is all about then," he added, taking Bill into his confidence.

Bill nodded again, more encouragingly this time.

"He'll be sorry he missed you," the burly man said. "You see, he made up his mind to go to England in pretty much of a hurry. This Lord Oliver wrote to him about a horse called Panic, a mean one. At first Finn turned him down but then Mr. Dancer heard about it. . . ."

"Mr. Dancer?" Bill asked. "I don't believe I know him."

"I guess you wouldn't at that. He's Finn's new backer. He put up the money to get him started in

New York. Anyway, when he heard Lord Oliver
wanted Panic tamed before the Queen of England
he insisted that they go if only for the publicity."

"I can understand that . . . knowing Finn," Bill
said. "I can also understand why he didn't want to
take on such a horse *alone*."

"Yeah," the other agreed knowingly. He turned
suddenly to a nearby stall where an ugly brown
horse was kicking savagely against the sides.
"Quiet!" he shouted angrily.

"Is that horse to be driven by Finn?" Bill asked.

The stable manager grinned. "Him? Finn tames
him 'bout twice a week. He's part of the act."

"How long do you work on him before he's
exhibited?" Bill asked without meeting the other's
eyes.

"Twenty-four hours without food or water usually
does it. Leaves enough fire in him to put on a good
show without makin' it too hard for Finn to get
control. He's a good subject, all right. I guess you
an' Finn never had one as good as him. He's real
ugly-lookin', scares the daylights out of people."

Bill Dailey turned away. "No, we didn't have any
like him," he replied. "C'mon, Hank."

"I'll tell Finn you were here," the stable manager
called after them.

"I'll tell him myself," Bill answered. "I'm stickin'
around."

Boss Horse-Tamer

13

That same week Bill Dailey rented a small livery stable on 61st Street. He announced to the public through the newspapers that he was prepared to help owners in "the education of their horses." He offered no extraordinary tricks and did not claim himself to be the "World's Greatest Horse-Tamer." Modestly he stated that although he had no more special fitness for this work than most people, having spent much time with horses he had gotten to know their ways and temperament. He could teach owners how best to get along with their horses and make them their friends.

For the first time in Bill Dailey's career there was little response to his offer of help. This could have been due either to his complete lack of showmanship or to a feeling, on the part of the people of New York City, that they had nothing more to learn from professed horse-tamers. The few who did employ him had horses with simple vices resulting from poor management. Bill had little trouble correcting them and they came and went without fanfare.

The New York *Standard* said of his work, "Professor Dailey spends more time educating owners than their horses." Such a statement did not bring more owners knocking on his door, for it seemed that New York horsemen did not like to be taught publicly.

At the end of two weeks Bill said, "I guess New York's not for us, Hank."

"Folks here don't want to be taught," his brother agreed. "They want entertainment."

"Maybe so. At least most of 'em seem to think there's no controlling a bad horse unless you have some magical powers."

"We're farm people," Hank said. "Let's go back to those who really *want* your help and need it."

"No, I'm stickin' around to see Finn."

"What good is it going to do even if you can expose him for what he is?"

"It might help some horses," Bill replied quietly.

"No one will believe you," his brother said. "He's too popular."

"In a way that's why intelligent horsemen aren't coming to us now with their problem horses. They've known too many men like Finn Caspersen. They're scared to trust a good horse to us for treatment. But some people might listen. And if I could prove to 'em . . . " His voice drifted off and his eyes were half-closed in his planning.

The next day the newspapers carried a glowing account of Finn Caspersen's conquest of Panic in England. As Bill said, it sounded exactly as if Finn had written the article himself.

PANIC TAMED

Before the Queen and Royal Family, Prof. Finn Caspersen yesterday subdued the notorious horse Panic, owned by Lord Oliver.

Panic had been vicious from the time he was a colt and was kept for breeding purposes at the Winchester Stud, forty-one miles from London, in a building erected especially for him. He was so vicious that he would scream when anyone approached and would attempt to smash his stall into lucifer matches. No one went near him, for he would destroy every living thing. Visitors used to throw articles into his brick box in order to see him fight. When he was fed or watered, the first procedure for his groom was to ascertain where the enemy stood by thrusting a long pole in the stable door; he would then deposit the food, shut the door and vanish as quickly as possible.

Prof. Caspersen changed all this in a moment, as it were. He ordered the stable door to be thrown open and introduced himself according to his system without delay. In a half-hour the indomitable Panic was ridden by a child, listened tranquilly to the beating of a drum in his ears and stood serene when an umbrella was flourished in his face. Gentle as a lamb, he followed his conqueror around the arena like a dog, stopping when Prof. Caspersen pointed his finger, lying down when told and rising again when permission was given. All these things were done by Panic in a mild, good-humored sort of way, as if the wish to oblige his master was the sole ruling motive.

The speedy, easy and complete success of Prof. Caspersen in this remarkable case has given him the most flattering and exalted reputation in England. He is truly the "Boss Horse-Tamer in the World" as claimed!

"That's awfully hard to believe," Hank told his brother.

"I don't believe it," Bill said thoughtfully, "not the part about Finn walkin' into the stall and

changing Panic the way it says he did, anyway. I
wonder what he's going to do next."

"Something pretty spectacular," Hank prophe-
sied. "You can bet your life on that."

They learned the next day how right Hank was.
According to the papers, Finn Caspersen had
purchased Panic from Lord Oliver and was returning to the United States with him. He would exhibit
him nightly at the largest arena in New York,
Niblo's Garden.

"Now we'll see," Bill Dailey said.

"I wonder," his brother commented. "I wonder."

Three weeks later Finn Caspersen arrived in
New York with Panic. Bill did not go to the pier to
witness Finn's homecoming. Instead he bided his
time and read about the thousands who were on
hand to welcome the "Boss Horse-Tamer of the
World." It seemed that Finn didn't want anyone to
see Panic before his opening at Niblo's Garden. He
had the notorious horse transported from ship to
stable in a closed red wagon with his name printed
in large letters on the side. However, Finn had no
objection to displaying the gifts he'd received from
his British admirers, including the Queen. They
were carried in an open carriage for all New York to
see.

Bill let another day go by before going to the
Garden stables. He had no trouble finding Finn. He

had only to look for the largest crowd. Finn was in
the center, his stovepipe hat higher than all the
others, his eyes reckless as ever, his voice singing
self-praise as he told the group of his successful trip.

". . . and Panic is seventeen hands of solid bone
and muscle," he boomed. "Never in your life will
you see a horse like him, gentlemen. Come tonight
and see our first show." His eyes found Bill Dailey
and disclosed neither shock nor surprise. "Now I
have some work to do, gentlemen," he said,
dismissing the group with a friendly wave of his big
hand.

When they were alone Bill Dailey said, "I see
you're still sellin' the Secret." There were boxes
of the taming medicine piled high against the wall.

"Yep. Doing pretty well, too." Finn grinned
good-naturedly and put a hand on Bill's shoulder.
"Let's stop beating each other over the head, shall
we, Bill? You lead your life, and I'll lead mine."

Bill Dailey shrugged off Finn's hand.

"Still touchy," the big man said, scowling. "Still
the pocket-sized Atlas, holding the world on your
shoulders."

"I just don't want to be friends."

"Don't worry about it," Finn said. "We won't
be."

"I suppose you've got a big iron muzzle for Panic

to wear tonight?"

"Sure. How'd you guess?"

"You tried to get me to do that back in Pitts-burgh. Remember?"

"I'd forgotten."

"An' a wild zebra. Did you get one of those too, Finn?"

"No, just Panic and some pretty ugly horses."

"How long did you tie Panic down before you gave your royal exhibition?"

For the first time Finn's temper flared, but he soon regained control of himself and grinned broad-ly. "I keep forgetting I owe what I am to you," he said.

It was Bill's turn to be enraged. "I never taught you *that*," he said furiously.

"But you told me how to weaken a horse," Finn pointed out. "Panic was a tough one, all right, as mean as they come. It took us ten full nights to break him and even then he was fairly roaring. We ended up leading him behind a dog cart to London and back, forty-one miles each way!"

"Who's *we?*"

"Mr. Dancer and me. He stayed in England." He paused to study Bill Dailey's face carefully. "I don't suppose you've changed your mind and would like to work with me. I've got it good, Bill, real good."

"You're having trouble, aren't you? You can't keep horses under control by fear alone. Have you found that out?"

Finn nodded.

Bill went on relentlessly. "You *had* to buy Panic, didn't you, knowing that Lord Oliver would discover his horse was no better than before once Panic regained his strength?"

"I wanted him anyway," Finn said defiantly. "Wait'll you see the crowd that comes to see him tonight. He's seventeen hands of solid gold!"

"I'll bet he is," Bill answered, turning to look at the closed stall behind them. "Have you an' your stable manager got him tied down now? How long has it been this time, Finn?"

Not waiting for an answer, Bill walked quickly toward the stall door. He was halfway there when Finn caught him by the shoulder and whirled him around.

"Get out of here," Finn said, "and get out fast!"

Bill clenched his fists, then opened them again. Fighting wasn't going to do any good, either for him or Panic or all the other horses Finn would work over if he wasn't stopped. There was only one place to expose Finn, and that was in the Garden ring. Bill was prepared to take that step during the evening performance. He had it all figured out.

Circus Ring

14

Bill Dailey went from the Garden to the Barnum and Bailey Circus quarters outside the city and found the man he wanted.

"You'll do it for me then?" the circus man asked anxiously. "You said you'd be back if you decided to do it."

Bill nodded. "But it has to be done my way."

"Any way you say, Professor, just as long as you do it. You know how much it means to me."

"It's just not in my line, that's all," Bill said.

"Yeah, that's what you said back in Reading. But listen, Professor, you're just helping me out. You like to help people with their animals, don't you? I heard you say so myself."

"I was talkin' about horses."

"This shouldn't be much different."

"I don't know. You said yourself it's never been successful before."

"That's why when you tame him for me I'll have the best act in the business. Mr. Barnum said he'd take it. He promised he would."

"I can't promise you I'll tame him. I'll do my best, that's all."

"From what I saw of your exhibition in Reading that's enough for me. Anyone who could tame Tar Heel . . ."

"It's not the same thing," Bill interrupted. "Have you bought him yet?"

"No, I was waiting for your answer. He's no good to me unless he's tamed."

"You'll have to take your chances then."

"Seven hundred dollars' worth of chances," the man agreed thoughtfully. "That's what he'll cost me. But he's cheap at the price if I can use him in the act. I couldn't buy him from the Park Zoo for five times that if he hadn't killed his caretaker an' crippled another. Think of him doing a thing like that, Professor."

"I am thinkin' of it," Bill answered.

" 'Course he wouldn't be a draw if he didn't have such a bad reputation," the man went on. "He's a

man-eater an' everybody in New York knows it. You
get him so I can drive him and I'll have the biggest
act in the business."

"You'll stop the show with him, all right," Bill
admitted.

"So let's go, Professor. Where you goin' to tame
him . . . at your place?"

"No, I don't want that kind of show in there. I'm
no circus man."

"That's what you said before. Where will it be
then?"

"We'll take him from the zoo directly to the
Garden," Bill answered.

"The *Garden?*" the man repeated, puzzled. "But
that's where Finn Caspersen's puttin' on his act."

"I know," Bill said quietly. "It's goin' to be quite a
show tonight . . . a double feature . . . an' no one
knows it, not even Finn."

Panic

15

Niblo's Garden was a huge circular building with a center ring and seats for several thousand spectators. That evening every seat was occupied, with an estimated crowd of a thousand more waiting outside.

Finn Caspersen stood alone in the center of the ring. He was dressed in his finest clothes—a pale gray suit, striped waistcoat and a gray silk topper—and as he held up a white-gloved hand in his best professional manner it was evident to the crowd that he wasn't going to do any horse taming immediately.

When his vast audience had quieted he said in a booming voice that would have been the envy of any

carnival man, "GENtlemen and HORsemen!
Welcome to the new home of Panic, the most
notorious horse in all Europe! It was the Queen of
England herself who proclaimed him untameable
and yet you will shortly see him come to me at call.
Yes, you will see this and much more. But first let
me tell you how his taming came about."

Solemnly Finn Caspersen removed his topper,
and his unruly blond hair shone in the flickering
light of the gas lamps.

"I have been among horses since I was twelve
years old, and at first had a great many accidents,"
he continued. "My every limb has been broken
except for this arm." He raised his right arm,
waving his hat in the air. "But because I was young
when these accidents happened the bones naturally
healed quickly. To prevent such things from occur-
ring again, however, I spent years devising the
world's best system of horse management. Now I
can make any horse conscious of my power . . .
make him gentle and even affectionate. Now I
know a horse's every thought and can break him of
whatever bad habits he may have.

"When I was exhibiting so successfully here the
London papers all wrote, 'It is all very well for you
to call yourself Boss Horse-Tamer of the World, but
try taming our Panic!' Of course I insisted upon

demonstrating my power over this horse. Lord Oliver, his owner, replied that Panic was so vicious that he could not be brought to me and that I must go to him. *And that I did,* traveling all the way to England, my friends!

"Now let me tell you that Panic had not been out of his box for three years. A brick stable had been built for him, and he would have been shot except that he was the last of a race of splendid-blooded horses and his owner was anxious to preserve him if at all possible. I found that by his biting and kicking he had so injured himself that he could not be taken out of his box, so I had to wait ten days for his recovery before I could exhibit my system upon him in public."

Finn Caspersen stopped to clear his throat and looked slowly around the huge arena. When he was convinced he held every single person's attention he continued. "Part of the time Panic wore a big iron muzzle and collar which his owner could get on him only by letting a rope down through the roof of his stall, fastening it under his neck and raising him off his forefeet. I tell you, gentlemen, Panic was a horrible sight to behold when I saw him biting and kicking and seeking to destroy every living thing in the neighborhood of his stall!"

Again Finn Caspersen stopped to survey his

audience and from far in the back someone yelled, "Tell us how you approached him then! What method did you use?"

Finn Caspersen smiled patiently, and then answered, "My own, of course. I have learned that horses have a reason for everything they do. I knew that if I approached Panic with a stick he would fight me as he had fought others who had come to whip him. In the box was a double door so that I could open the upper half and leave the bottom closed. I went quietly, and opened it noiselessly. Panic turned around, saw me, started back violently but did not attempt to ravage me as he had others. After a while he came slowly up to smell me and, in spite of Lord Oliver's entreaties, I stood still and rubbed a bit of my Arabian Secret on his muzzle."

Finn stopped for the full effect of his words to register upon his audience.

"Presently," he went on, "when I saw that Panic was standing quietly, I began to fondle him. Lord Oliver begged me to tie his head and I did so. You never saw such fighting when Panic found himself tied! Realizing that he would either kill himself or tear down the box, I released him at once and began all over again. After he allowed me to fondle him I took him into the straw-yard and proceeded as with any horse until at last he would let me take any liberty with him. Lord Oliver mounted him with impunity and rode him before the Queen and the Royal Family in great style, proving to her and to all England—yes, to all Europe—that I was everything claimed for me, the Boss Horse-Tamer of the World, and as celebrated for my taming as Panic had been for his viciousness!"

Finn put on his silk topper and raised his hands high in the air, prompting the thunderous cheers that followed.

When the applause ended Finn turned to the ring entrance. "Now, gentlemen," he said, "I shall exhibit before you the most renowned horse in all Europe! Here, appearing for the very first time in America, is the one and only Panic!"

A great chestnut horse wearing an iron muzzle was led into the ring. Finn took him from his stable manager and proudly exhibited him for all to see.

To the eyes of the experienced horsemen in the crowd there was no doubt that this golden horse was of the finest blood and capable of great sensitivity and courage as well as prolonged resistance when excited. His head was well proportioned; he was wide and full between the eyes and long of nasal bone. His eyelids were thin and the distance from eyes to ears was noticeably short. His ears, of course, indicated his fine blood. They were exceedingly fine and pointed, and were set close together.

"I have not treated him since leaving England," Finn Caspersen told his huge audience, "but despite that you will see him give me his foot like a gentleman."

Finn touched the horse's right foreleg and Panic raised it quickly. Finn walked about the ring and Panic followed him like a dog, stopping when Finn pointed a finger at him. Then the man would say something and Panic would lie down immediately, waiting for another command before jumping to his feet. Next Finn got a drum and beat it vigorously, the horse showing neither fear nor alarm. Much the same thing happened when Finn opened and closed a large umbrella before Panic's eyes and then held it over his head.

The crowd cheered wildly, for this was truly an impressive exhibition of docility for a horse who had had the worst reputation in all Europe.

Finn Caspersen turned Panic over to his stable manager and then said to his audience, "Now I shall exhibit another horse sent to me for taming. I shall subject him to the same method of treatment that I used upon Panic. You will then see with your very own eyes how such a feat was accomplished." He removed his fine gray coat and silk topper, putting them to one side. He poured some Arabian Secret on his hands, rubbing it in slowly and then, dramatically, turning toward the ring entrance. Now he waited for his stable manager to bring the next horse into the ring, the ugly brown one they had prepared for tonight's performance.

But instead of the brown horse a red circus wagon was backed into the ring.

"What's this?" Finn shouted, when the wagon came to a stop, blocking the entrance. "Tom!" he called out to his stable manager.

The crowd was cheering Finn Caspersen again. A closed circus wagon. There was suspense for you! What manner of horse was inside? It was the kind of show they had come to expect from Finn. They applauded all the more, urging him to open the door of the wagon.

"Tom!" Finn called again. There was no way for him to leave the ring graciously. Suddenly there was a scurrying of feet on the roof of the wagon. He looked up hopefully. "Tom, what is . . ." He stopped abruptly.

Bill Dailey sat on the edge of the roof, swinging his legs slightly. "Sure, Finn, go ahead an' open the door," he said "Don't keep your audience waitin'."

"What are you trying to do?"

Bill answered, "Open up and see."

"Don't be silly."

"I'm not being silly. They're all watchin' you, Finn, and waiting. I'm just here for the ride. Here's a chance to prove you're all you claim to be. No one's touched this case before. He's mean an' needs a lot of taming."

"You think I'm a fool?" Finn asked nervously. He swept a hand across his wet brow. Was there no way out of this? "Where's Tom?" His breathing was heavy, his face drawn.

"A couple of circus men are handling him."

"What's inside this wagon?"

"A surprise, Finn, a real surprise for you an' your audience."

"I don't like surprises."

"I know. I don't think you'll like this one, either."

"Why are you doing this to me?"

"I told you I'd be back to expose you."

The big man's eyes shifted uneasily like those of a wild animal at bay. The noise of the crowd rose to a high demanding pitch. It was time for him to do something—either run for it or open the red door and take his chances.

"Give me a break, Bill," he pleaded.

"The kind of break you gave Panic and all the other horses you've worked over?"

"I *tried* to do it your way, Bill. But some people—and I'm one of 'em—just don't have the hands for it. You've got to admit that, Bill."

"Not hands, Finn, *head*. Head and heart are needed to manage horses. You've got neither."

"If *you've* got heart, give me a break, Bill," Finn pleaded once more. "These people will . . ."

"They certainly will," Bill agreed, "when they find out you've been foolin' them all along."

Angry blows against wood came from inside the wagon and the crowd roared louder.

"Let's see what you got inside, Finn!" someone shouted. The urgent request was echoed by others. "Open up!" the crowd cried. "Open up!"

"Sure, go ahead," Bill prodded the big man. "You got your show, a real circus act even to the wagon. That's what you wanted, wasn't it?"

Finn Caspersen became more frightened than he'd ever been in his life. He listened to the savage thumps coming from the closed wagon and said in panic, "All right, Bill, you win. W-What do you want me to do? How do I get out of this?"

"I want you to come and work for me again."

"You want me to *what?*"

"I want you where I can watch you," Bill said decisively. "You're not goin' to touch a horse ever again, if I can help it. Nor are you goin' to sell any more secret taming medicines or cure-alls. You've got to promise. . . ."

"I'm not promising anything," the big man said with sudden defiance.

"I think you will, Finn, an' it won't take long for you to make up your mind." Bill Dailey suddenly jumped down to the ring, landing lightly on the balls of his feet.

"What are you going to do?"

"Open this door for you."

Finn Caspersen bit his heavy lower lip. "But you just said you didn't want me to touch another horse," he reminded Bill as a last resort. The persistent chant of the crowd had become deafening.

"This isn't a horse," Bill answered, opening the door.

Man-Eater!

16

The wagon had a double door and Bill opened only the lower half. "When he shows his head, catch hold of the halter strap on your side," Bill told Finn.

"Not me," the big man answered. "You won't catch me. . . ."

"You'd better. The only chance we have to get out of this ring alive is to keep him between us."

Finn Caspersen froze in terror and Bill Dailey prodded him hard. "Get ready," he warned. "He'll be pushin' his head out any second now. Funny thing, Finn, I got the halter on him the same way I did with Wild Bess. Or don't you remember her? She was the first case you got me. She chased me over the haymow rail, an' I got a rope halter on her by usin' a long stick. Remember now? Or is that goin' too far back for you?"

Whatever Finn Caspersen had been about to say died on his lips, for suddenly an ugly head appeared in the doorway. There was a long leather strap attached to either side of the halter.

"Now," Bill said. "Grab! I'm opening the top of the door!"

The wild African mountain zebra would have stopped any show or circus. There was no one in the vast arena, including Bill Dailey, who did not feel a tremor of fear run through his body at the sight of him.

"When he comes," Bill warned, "keep him between us. Here's a chance to throw your weight around."

Finn as well as most of the spectators knew the evil reputation of this animal. He was the only zebra in New York, having been captured a few months before in northeast Africa, and was the largest of his species. He had killed one zoo keeper and crippled several others. The newspapers had nicknamed him Man-Eater.

Many in the crowd got to their feet and made for the exits. There was too little separating them from this wild beast—only a low rail and two men.

Man-Eater's long ears, fringed with dirty hair,

were swept back hard against his head. His eyes were bloodshot and gleamed like balls of fire. His black-striped body trembled with his mounting rage at being held in captivity. He was grotesquely ugly, low-necked, pot-bellied and filthy.

Without taking his eyes off the zebra, Finn said, "Get me out of here and I'll promise you anything."

"Hold on, then. Here he comes!"

The beast sprang at them with open mouth and vicious-looking teeth. He made directly for Finn and Bill pulled hard, trying to upset him. The zebra's head came around with a snap but he did not lose his balance and fall.

"Hold him, Finn!" Bill cried.

The savage eyes bore down on Bill and for a terrifying second he thought that Finn had bolted, leaving him alone. Then the zebra was brought to an abrupt stop by the big man. Bill jumped away, then quickly wound his strap around the zebra's haunches. When the ugly head was being pulled in Finn's direction Bill yanked hard, throwing the zebra off balance. Down the beast went on one knee. Bill pulled again, rolling him over. But before he could do anything else the zebra had jumped to his feet and was charging Finn!

Dropping his strap, Finn ran from the ring. The big man went over the rail flying, landing in the first row of seats which had already been vacated. Bill stopped the zebra but then the beast turned on him!

When the attack came Bill too had no alternative but to run. Still holding the strap, he moved in a tight, fast circle with the zebra after him. He tried to catch hold of the long, ropelike tail but couldn't. Then he threw himself hard against the striped body, trying to pull the vicious head around. But he was not heavy enough to throw the animal off balance and slipped and almost fell. As he moved forward again he felt Finn's loose strap encircle his legs. He tried to jump clear of it but the zebra moved at the same time, pulling the dangling strap taut. Bill found himself falling.

Man-Eater!

Desperately Bill tried to catch hold of the short-maned neck to keep the snapping teeth away from him. He succeeded in grabbing the hair just as something heavy landed on the zebra's haunches from the roof of the red circus wagon which was alongside. The blow knocked the beast off balance and he went down hard, falling beside Bill. Then somebody was astride him, half on, half off, and Bill heard his brother's voice.

"I got hold of his tail. Tie it quick!"

Bill realized then that it was Hank who had leaped from the wagon roof onto the zebra. Quickly

he tied the halter strap to the hairy end of the tail and they jumped away together.

The zebra staggered to his feet, the strap having been left slack enough to allow for this. He turned around slowly at first as if uncertain what he should attack. Then he went faster, following the pull on his head and fighting himself without knowing it. He spun crazily and in a short time fell over. Within a moment he had jumped up again and was turning as rapidly as before.

Bill and Hank had moved to the other side of the ring. In common with the vast, silent crowd they watched the furious animal spin like a pinwheel. In his frenzy and frustration he looked uglier than ever. His thick body had the oily smoothness of a snake. But he had none of a snake's craftiness. His temper had risen to fever pitch and he turned faster, spending all his strength and energy fighting himself without knowing it.

Bill said, "It won't be long now." The zebra's determination to resist until completely exhausted was all Bill had hoped for. Without pain or injury, the zebra would spin until he could be brought under control and handled.

They lost track of the time but finally, wavering and about to fall, the zebra came to an unsteady stop. Bill went to him quickly and caught hold of the halter. Now it was time to go to work again. The small glazed eyes were turned his way but the beast made no attempt to ravage or resist. Bill ran his hands over the thick neck, steadying him and speaking kindly to him. Finally he untied the strap from the zebra's tail.

The crowd watched in stunned silence. Finn Caspersen got to his feet and straightened his clothes. Someone pointed to him and laughed. It broke the tension and more laughter followed. It was echoed by thunderous applause for Bill Dailey.

"You done?" Hank asked his brother, coming up beside him.

"For now."

"Will he stay this way?"

"If I keep working with him. But go get Finn now. Tell him we're leavin'. The show's over." As Hank started to leave the ring Bill called him back. "And thanks for doin' what you did. It took a lot of nerve."

Hank Dailey hurried on, his face flushed with pride. He'd never tell his brother that he hadn't jumped from the wagon roof on purpose. *He'd fallen*. But maybe he would have jumped anyway.

"I guess that's about all there is to it," Henry Dailey said, finishing his story and rising from the straw in the stable. "Now I'm an old man and can't look a zebra in the face without thinkin' of the one I sat on at Niblo's Garden."

"Did your brother keep him tame?" Alec asked.

"Up to a point. He got the zebra to pull the circus man around in a cart but the man was never truly safe. Man-Eater made Bill's reputation, though. After that, there wasn't a soul in the country who didn't want his help with difficult horses. Bill became the best horse-tamer there ever was. He even wrote a book about it to reach those he couldn't visit personally. He was a big man, all right . . . even for a little guy."

Alec went over to the Black Stallion and rubbed him thoughtfully. "What became of Finn Caspersen? He was quite a character. Did he stay with your brother as he promised he'd do?"

"For a while."

"You mean he ran out on him again?"

"Well, not exactly. What I mean is that he never went back to treatin' horses. He knew Bill wouldn't have stood for that. No, Finn got hold of another way of makin' a living and it suited him just fine. He made a fortune at it."

"What was it?"

"Selling bicycles."

"Bicycles?" Alec repeated, puzzled. "What was

so great about *them*?"

"These were extra-special bicycles. You see, Finn figured that a bicycle craze was about to sweep New York. He decided that if girls were bein' allowed to ride horseback alone in the park, even more of 'em would soon be ridin' bicycles. It would give 'em a chance to wear sporty clothes and slenderize at the same time.

"It turned out that way, too," Henry continued thoughtfully. "Finn even sold a bike to Lillian Russell—that was the showgirl my brother thought was so pretty, the one at the Casino Theater on Broadway. It was a gold-plated bike with mother-of-pearl handlebars on which her monogram was engraved in diamonds and emeralds. Even the hubs and spokes were set with jewels that used to sparkle in the sun when she rode by."

"You mean you saw her?"

"I sure did," Henry replied dreamily.

"But Finn couldn't have sold many of that kind of bike," Alec said.

"No, but he made enough in the business to start sellin' electric carriages that went as fast as eleven miles an hour! They sure scared a lot of horses and as a result my brother was busier than ever."

"Was that the last you heard of Finn?"

"Oh, no, I saw him after that. A few years later

when I returned to New York alone I saw him drivin' one of the craziest things I'd ever seen in my life up to that time. It was called a devil wagon."

"What did it do?"

Henry pulled on a piece of straw. "It was one of the first *gasoline* carriages, Alec, and Finn was selling 'em. He advertised that they were 'noiseless, odorless, and perfectly safe and controllable, as most horses aren't!' He even predicted they'd soon be in general use. Finn was the laughingstock of New York because of his wild claims, so when he passed me I laughed at him too. I even yelled with the others, '*Get a horse!*' "

The Black Stallion snorted and they turned to him, smiling.

Alec said, "I guess what the Black means is that Finn had the last laugh."

"Maybe so," Henry answered. "But I don't think even Finn dreamed we'd be flying our horse across the Atlantic Ocean." He made for the door. "C'mon, let's see if they're ready to go yet."

ABOUT THE AUTHOR

Walter Farley's love for horses began when he was a small boy living in Syracuse, New York, and continued as he grew up in New York City, where his family moved. Unlike most city children, he was able to fulfill this love through an uncle who was a professional horseman. Young Walter spent much of his time with this uncle, learning about the different kinds of horse training and the people associated with each.

Walter Farley began to write his first book, *The Black Stallion*, while he was a student at Brooklyn's Erasmus Hall High School and Mercersburg Academy in Pennsylvania. He finished it and had it published while he was still an undergraduate at Columbia University.

The appearance of *The Black Stallion* brought such an enthusiastic response from young readers that Mr. Farley went on to write more stories about the Black, and about other horses as well. He now has twenty-five books to his credit, including his first dog story, *The Great Dane Thor*, and his story of America's greatest thoroughbred, *Man o' War*. His books have been enormously successful in this country, and have also been published in fourteen foreign countries.

When not traveling, Walter Farley and his wife, Rosemary, divide their time between a farm in Pennsylvania and a beach house in Florida.